FILTHY *beautiful* LIES

FILTHY BEAUTIFUL LIES
BOOK 1

New York Times & USA Today Bestselling Author
KENDALL RYAN

About the Book

I have no idea why she auctioned off her virginity for a cool mil. Regardless, I'm now the proud new owner of a perfectly intact hymen. A lot of good that will do me. I have certain tastes, certain sexual proclivities. My cock is a bit more discriminatory than most. And training a virgin takes finesse and patience – both of which I lack.

Sophie Evans has been backed into a corner. With her sister's life hanging in the balance, the only choice is to claw her way out, even if that means selling her virginity to the highest bidder at an exclusive erotic club. When Colton Drake takes her home, she quickly learns nothing is as it seems with this beautiful and intense man. Being with him poses challenges she never expected, and pushes her to want things she never anticipated.

A sinfully seductive erotic romance where everything has a price and the cost of love is the highest of all from New York Times & USA Today bestselling author, Kendall Ryan.

PROLOGUE

Tonight I will be sold to the highest bidder. As I stand here in this quiet room, I try to find that little voice of reason telling me I'm doing the right thing. She's nowhere to be found. *Traitorous whore.*

I meet my dim blue gaze in the mirror and remind myself that I'm entering into this arrangement knowingly, and by choice. Not the choice I *want* to make, certainly not my life's ambition, but it's a choice I *have* to make in order to save someone I love.

In another hour I will belong to someone—a man with sick needs and fetishes that propel him to purchase his companion rather than date a normal girl.

Heaven help me.

CHAPTER ONE

Sophie

I've been told that I could go for more than two hundred and fifty thousand dollars, and maybe more given that I'm still a virgin.

The money will mean the difference between life and death for my twin sister and best friend in the whole world. It will mean I can pay the fees to get her into the experimental treatment program for advance stage ovarian cancer. We're both just twenty-one years old and have barely lived. When she got cancer at age nineteen and had a hysterectomy, I promised her I'd carry her babies someday, a promise I intended to keep. And now she's facing death in a matter of months if I don't intervene, which is why I'm standing in the dimly lit dressing room applying my third coat of mascara and dressed only in a pair of panties.

I'd found out about this place completely by coincidence. A few weeks ago, I would have never believed places like this existed. I'd been searching online for money making schemes—something, *anything*, that could help me raise the three hundred thousand dollars we needed. My parents made ends meet, but just barely. So I knew it was up to me. My job searches turned out to be a joke. My skills could earn me minimum wage at best, maybe waiting tables. That's when my internet searches got more interesting and my attitude bolder.

I agreed to an interview at a high-end strip club. As if the interview itself wasn't embarrassing enough—being asked to undress in front of the club's owner and prove my non-existent dancing abilities. But when he'd asked how much money I hoped to make dancing and I said three hundred thousand dollars in the next few months, he'd laughed in my face and told me to get dressed. It was obvious to us both that based on my dancing skills, I'd never earn that kind of money. Let alone in my small Northern California town.

When he saw the tears swimming in my eyes and inquired about why I needed the money, I'd given him, a complete stranger, the entire sad story. Once I was dressed, he brought me into his office and made me promise that what he was about to say would stay only between us. The shifty way his eyes danced around the room told me whatever it was, it probably wasn't legal. I didn't care. I'd never so much as run a red light, but I was willing to do anything—go to any extreme to save Becca. I promised him complete secrecy.

He asked how serious I was about saving my sister and warned that I wouldn't like what he was about to tell me. That was how I learned about tonight's auction.

Bill, the strip club owner, entered me into tonight's bids. He'd arranged everything for a ten percent cut in my earnings. I'd seen a doctor, who tested me for pregnancy and STDs, and verified my virginity. Bill had also made me an appointment at a local salon for full body waxing and a makeover—a haircut with long layers and caramel highlights in my otherwise chestnut brown hair, along with a manicure and a pedicure. All of which would come out of my earnings too. If I didn't sell, I would be responsible for paying him back. But Bill all but guaranteed I'd sell. He said that virgins were very rare and that someone so natural and beautiful would go for a high price. I just hope to keep my nerves under control so that I can actually follow through with this. I feel like throwing up and I haven't even eaten all day.

I turn to the sound of a light tapping on my door and Bill pokes his head in. My arms fly over my chest as I try to cover my breasts. My modesty is pointless and a hysterical giggle bubbles up in my throat. All too soon I'll be exposed to a roomful of men and expected to give my body to one of them, but I focus on maintaining my innocence while I still can. Bill raises an eyebrow at me. "Are you ready?"

I glance in the mirror one last time and draw a steadying breath. I look down at my toned legs, thanks to hours spent jogging—my only form of stress relief—to my stomach that is a bit softer than I would like, to my breasts that jiggle when I move. The eyes looking back at me are harder than before. *Good.* I will need that hard exterior to survive the next six months.

I hadn't known this side of the world existed and now I'm entering into it. I'm doing this for Becca, I remind myself. Drawing every ounce of strength I can, I uncross my arms from over my breasts and nod to Bill. "I'm ready."

His eyes give me a cursory once over. I'm grateful he doesn't leer. "You look great. Very natural. That should work in your favor," he remarks, leading me from the safety of the small dressing room. I'm not sure I'm ready for whatever waits for me beyond.

But I see what he means as we progressed down the hallway. There are a few other women ranging from early twenties to late thirties and each of them seemed to have embraced the stripper look—big hair and layers of thick makeup, red stained lips, fishnet stockings and sky high heels. All of them are wearing g-strings. I'd been told the only article of clothing allowed was a pair of panties so I'd chosen my most modest pair—light blue briefs with lace along the hem. They're cute and feminine and comfortable. It had never occurred to me to try and make myself look sexier. Regret churns in my stomach. What if no one wants me? I'll have done all this for nothing, plus owe Bill for the expensive makeover he provided. The concrete floor against my bare feet sends an icy chill up my body, pebbling my nipples into hardened points. My arms once again cross over my chest as I clutch my breasts.

I might be more covered than the other women, but somehow I feel *more* exposed. Completely ripped open for the world to see. I'm dressed as *me*, not some sexified version of myself that I can portray to the men waiting on the other side of that door. Suddenly I don't want them to see the real me. I wanted to be caked in makeup with perhaps a long blonde wig and tassels hanging from my nipples. I could be whoever they wanted me to be. Instead I'm just Sophie and that seems much more dangerous to me. I can't let my new owner get inside my head. He might be buying the rights to my body, but he'll certainly never have the real me. I need to remember that.

When we stop outside a steel door, panic courses through my veins and my throat constricts, my gag reflex threatening to send bile shooting up my throat. I draw a deep breath through my nose and open my mouth to tell Bill I've changed my mind when his hand suddenly reaches out and twists the doorknob.

The door swings open to reveal a large, dimly lit room. The only light comes from a bare bulb that hangs directly above a platform-like stage in the center of the room. A dozen or so men sit in lounge chairs facing the small round stage, their faces completely hidden in the shadows. I'm unable to distinguish a single feature, which I know is the point. The nature of tonight's activities means they want their anonymity. And the kind of money that would be spent tonight bought them that right.

Bill gives me a gentle shove forward and whispers something of encouragement, but the blood pounding in my ears garbles the message.

My feet move across the room, my arms still crossed in a death grip across my breasts. The faint smell of cigar smoke assaults my senses as I move toward the platform. I keep my eyes trained on the floor, letting the swath of light from the single bulb hanging overhead draw me forward. My knees shake as I walk the final few steps. Nerves and a misplaced sense of duty propel me forward.

Finally I step onto the raised platform and face the small group of men. Keeping my eyes downcast, I know in this moment I would have never been brave enough to strip for a whole audience. I can barely stand here without my knees knocking together and just remembering to pull air into my lungs and release it again seems beyond my abilities. But a spike of determination rips through me. I'm here to save Becca.

A man standing in the shadows at the side of the room clears his throat. "I give you the ninth and final girl of the evening. And trust me when I tell you, gentlemen, that we've saved the best for last. She's as pure and untouched as they come. She comes to us as a virgin, willing, ready, and fully in agreement with the six-month terms. Now, who'd like to start the bidding?"

It's quiet for just a heartbeat and I wait for something to happen.

"Move your hands off your tits, angel," a man in the crowd says.

I raise my eyes toward the sound of the voice, but my hands stay where they are. A streak of defiance I didn't know I had rears its head. No one owns me yet. Not a single bid had been placed. I still control my destiny.

I shift my weight, feeling that tingling sensation that means my foot is falling asleep and clutch my chest tighter as though I'm hanging on for dear life. My heart races in my chest and little beads of sweat form under my arms despite the cool temperature in the room. I feel dizzy. Disoriented. But I tell myself can do this. I have to do this.

"Two hundred." The man's voice who'd ordered me to uncover myself places the first bid. I hope that's two hundred thousand and not two hundred dollars. It never occurred to me that I needed to have a minimum established before this began. I was not sleeping with some weird old man for two hundred dollars. But then I recalled Bill saying something about six figure minimums, and I relax the tiniest bit.

"Two fifty," another voice says. He sounds younger and has a slight Spanish accent.

"Three hundred," a third voice croaks.

Soon the price is up to five-seventy five and I feel faint listening to the whole exchange. I need to get off this stage before I pass out or throw up, or do something equally as terrifying, like go home with one of these sick men.

Be strong, Soph.

I draw another breath.

"Six hundred thousand," my tit-loving admirer counters. I don't want to go to the man who I've already defied by refusing to show my chest. Knowing my luck, his first order of business will be to punish me for that act of disobedience.

"Greedy tonight. He already has one and now he wants a second," the announcer chuckles.

The man who is currently driving up my price has apparently already purchased one girl tonight and now he wants me too. Call me old fashioned, but I always assumed I'd be the only slave in this type of arrangement. I thought I was signing up for the typical one man—one woman experience. This wasn't how I imagined losing my virginity, but I certainly never pictured being part of an orgy, or whatever he had planned. It disturbs me to think that he could buy us like cattle and force us to do things to each other and him. This whole process is going from bad to worse.

I look up and to the center of the room—to the one man who's remained completely silent so far. He crosses his ankle over his knee and leans back further in his chair, concealing his face entirely in the shadows. His casual, aloof behavior strikes something in me. I have a roomful of men bidding on my virginity, but somehow I don't like the idea that this one man isn't interested. Is there something wrong with me? It's self-conscious and stupid, but something about being mostly nude in a roomful of strangers puts bizarre thoughts in your head.

No one has countered the man to my left—the one who'd called me angel and wanted to see my breasts and my stomach churns in knots. He's offered six hundred thousand dollars, more than enough to pay for my sister's medical treatment, give Bill his ten percent and the money he spent on me at the salon. I should feel happy and relieved. This is what I wanted, right? But the idea of actually leaving with him and the other girl he's bought tonight sets off a gnawing feeling inside my chest.

"If there are no other bids…" the announcer begins.

My windpipe threatens to close. It can't end like this…

"Seven hundred," the man directly in front of me says. His voice is smooth and rich. Deep and hypnotic somehow. I lean forward on my toes trying to see his face. The foot he's crossed over his ankle bounces as he fidgets, the only sign he's now engaged in this bidding war. My heart leaps in my chest, doubling its pace as I wait nervously to see what will happen.

Not being able to discern anything else in the room, I focus on his shoe. It is large, a black shiny leather, and expensive-looking dress shoe. But I suppose you have to be insanely wealthy to buy another human being for the prices these men are offering. His foot twitches again and my eyes shoot up to where I imagine his face is.

The other man grumbles something under his breath, and I catch the word *overpriced*. Then he barks out another bid. "Seven twenty-five."

Crap. I don't want to be part of this weirdo's threesome fetish and I have no idea if going with

Mr. Shiny Dress Shoes will be any better, but I stare straight ahead, silently pleading with him to up the bid. A dose of raw willpower keeps me steady on my feet.

"One million dollars," he says after what feels like an eternity.

My head spins and I feel woozy. A million dollars? For me? There is no way I'm worth that as a sex slave. Once he realizes how inexperienced I am—not just at sex, but at everything—he'll have buyer's remorse, and maybe even try and return me. Yet still, I hold my breath, praying that no one will outbid him. Something inside me—woman's intuition, a gut feeling, tells me that out of all these men here tonight, I am supposed to go home with him, but the thought of actually giving myself over to one of these monsters for six months is terrifying.

I have nothing to go on but a clean, sleek, black leather shoe... but he gives off a good vibe. Maybe at the very least I'd be well taken care of. Panic threatens to overwhelm me. *Breath, Soph.*

"She's yours. No pussy's worth that much," the other man bites out, shifting in his seat.

My lungs fill with oxygen as I pull in a much

needed breath, filling my chest cavity.

"Our final object up for auction has been sold. Gentlemen, thank you for your participation tonight. If you would kindly make your way to the lounge area through the rear door to finalize payments and collect your earlier purchases. Drinks are available and some in-house entertainment if you're in the mood."

The announcer's voice buzzes in my head.

I've been sold.

Men rise from their chairs and I hear footsteps retreat as they exit the room. A door closes in the distance, leaving just my new master and me alone in the silent room. He hasn't moved at all.

I want to step down off the humiliating stage I've been made to stand on. I want my clothes. But I remain rooted in place, realizing for the first time that my actions are no longer my own.

"Come forward," he commands.

I swallow and step down off the platform, my legs heavy from standing in one spot for so long. I take slow strides across the room like I'm approaching a dangerous animal. Maybe I am. What kind of man buys a woman?

"I won't hurt you," he encourages and I take another tentative step closer, stopping directly in front of his chair. "Lights," he says to no one in particular and the overhead lights all flick on at once. Blinking several times against the sudden rush of light, my eyes remain downcast as they struggle to adjust.

Disoriented, I continue looking down, studying his shoes, which are now both resting squarely on the floor. "Look at me," he says.

I lift my chin and take in the man seated before me. Black suit. White crisp shirt. Black silk tie knotted loosely at his neck.

I inhale again, forcing another breath into my lungs and finally look into the eyes of the man who has just spent one million dollars to purchase me. Sky blue eyes fringed in heavy black lashes stare back at me, stealing the breath from my lungs. He is stunning. Tall, fit, and attractive. Confusion washes over me. What is a man like this doing here? He could walk into any bar in America and pick up a girl easily enough. My stomach twists in recognition. That can only mean that his tastes are peculiar enough that he requires complete obedience. He'll want things no normal girl would do. Oh god, I feel like I'm going to pass out. I can't let this attractive monster lure me in.

"Just breathe," he says, calming my fears.

I obey like a good little slave, opening my mouth and sucking in air greedily.

"That's it," he says soothingly, his own posture relaxing just slightly. "What should I call you?"

It's an interesting way to phrase the question. He didn't ask me for my name. Maybe he's assuming I'll give him a fake identity. And I probably would have if I'd been thinking clearly. Instead I whisper, "Sophie." As soon as it's off my lips, I momentarily regret giving him my real name. But then I realize I'll be living with him for six months and I don't think I can keep up with the lie of a fake identity that entire time. I'll already be lying to my family and friends about where I am. No sense making this even more difficult on myself.

He tilts his head to the side, continuing to study me. "Call me Drake," he says finally. I wonder if Drake is his real name.

Just when I'm beginning to think he's going to make me stand here all night, he rises from the chair. Having his full height in front of me is daunting. I'm average height, and he's at least a foot taller than me, well over six feet. I stagger back a step.

"Come with me." He turns and heads toward the exit and like an obedient pet, I follow closely behind him.

When we reach the steel door I entered through just thirty minutes before, it feels like I'm exiting as a whole different person. Drake turns to face me before opening the door. "Would you like my jacket?"

I look down at myself—at my pale blue panties that now feel childish and my hands which haven't strayed from my breasts. I nod weakly.

Shrugging out of his jacket, he's even more muscular than I first realized. His tailored dress shirt clings to his broad shoulders and defined chest. It sends a ripple of fear through my gut. Yes, he's attractive, but he's also strong. Which means I'll stand zero chance of defending myself against him if he gets too rough.

Ignoring my visual inspection of his body, he places the jacket over my shoulders, closing the lapels over my chest and buttoning the first button. I thought he might demand to see me, to inspect me for himself, but he only seems concerned with getting us the hell out of here. Which is fine by me.

Once I'm covered by the jacket, I let my hands

fall away and lower my arms, my stiff joints crying out from being in the same position for so long. My arms hang uselessly at my sides and I follow him out into the hall. As grateful as I am for his jacket, I can't mistake this first bit of kindness from him for more than it is. He doesn't want other men's eyes on something he's just purchased for himself.

We pass several others on the way out and I keep my eyes on Drake's shoes as I follow him down the hall, a false sense of security settling over me.

CHAPTER TWO

Sophie

He stops outside the dressing room I used earlier. "Are your clothes in there?"

I nod and mumble an unintelligible reply.

"Get dressed," he commands, his tone smooth.

I duck my head and push my way inside the small changing room. Once inside, I cannot keep my eyes from darting toward the mirror where I stood applying mascara just a short time ago. I can already see that the girl looking back at me is someone different. The black suit coat swallows me up, proclaiming me to belong to someone other than myself.

I shrug it off my shoulders, but not before taking a second to appreciate the fine feel of the feather light wool between my fingers and the crisp scent of cologne lightly permeating the fabric. There's something masculine and evocative about the jacket and I can't help but think about his deeper meaning behind him dressing me in it. Like a dog marking his territory with his scent.

Shaking the thought away, I fold the jacket neatly and step into my clothes—a pair of jeans, and a long sleeved cotton top, paired with ballet flats. I feel marginally better once I'm back in my old clothes. Stuffing my makeup bag into my purse, I loop it across my body and turn toward the mirror. I take one last look in the mirror, mentally preparing myself to face him again, and say a silent goodbye to the girl standing before me.

I pause at the doorway, my hand resting on the knob. It's now or never. I can either go and find Bill, beg to be let out of this contract, and deal with the consequences, or I can walk out of this room, and accept what I have to do. Either way, I know my life is going to change.

Straightening my spine and stealing an anxious breath into my lungs, I push open the door.

I meet Drake in the hall where he's standing waiting for me with a bored expression.

I feel his eyes quickly survey my new ensemble and I suddenly feel underdressed next to this wealthy and powerful man with his expensive suit and shiny shoes. He takes the jacket from me and begins walking toward the exit without a word. I'm expected to follow, so I do. I scurry to keep up with his long legs and powerful strides that eat up the concrete.

Once in the parking lot behind the building, I scan the few cars left in the lot, trying to memorize their license plates just in case he turns out to be a psycho — at least I'll have some piece of information to go to the police with, since I'm pretty sure his real name's not Drake.

The motorcycle he stops beside is unexpected and causes a little ripple of fear to cascade through me.

Drake puts his suit coat in the compartment under the seat and removes an extra helmet for me. His thumb smoothes away the worry line etched across my forehead. "You'll be safe," he says, and places the helmet on my head. The weight of it against my scalp is foreign. This will be my first time on a motorcycle. Apparently I'm in for a lot of firsts tonight.

After securing his own helmet, he climbs on

the bike and holds out his hand to help me. The warmth of his large palm against my own startles me. I swallow a wave of nerves, then I swing one leg over the seat and position myself behind him. The angle of the narrow seat causes me to slide forward until my chest is pressed against his firm back. There's no room for anything but close contact between us. The intimacy is unsettling.

I briefly wonder if he's designed it this way—bringing his bike rather than a car to show me right from the beginning that I have no control and to get used to close physical contact. Because surely a man who could spend one million dollars owns a car, if not several. Something in his quiet and serious nature tells me everything he does is deliberate and my mind is cataloging all of these things to piece together the puzzle of the man to whom I now belong to.

He kick starts the bike and my arms fly around his middle. I feel his chest rumble and I'm pretty sure he just chuckled at my response.

We pick up speed as he takes the on-ramp for the highway and the chilly night air rushing past my face cools the heat that lingers between our two bodies. I squeeze my eyes closed in an attempt to escape the panicky feeling rising in my chest, but all it does is make my motion sickness kick in and I open my eyes once again. He accelerates and I cling to him desperately, linking my fingers in front of his tight abdomen.

Just as I'm praying we don't have a long trip on this bike, he begins to slow and I look up to see that we're on a service drive in the middle of a dark field. My senses are on high alert as I wonder what we're doing out here in the middle of nowhere.

I never imagined we'd fly somewhere, so when we pull up alongside a small private jet parked on an abandoned airstrip, bitter acid burns its way up my throat.

Panic zips through my veins at the thought of leaving everything I know behind. Even my zip code, which had never really meant that much to me, suddenly feels like something that defines me, is being ripped away.

Without so much as a carry-on bag, I follow him up the narrow set of stairs leading into the belly of the plane. It's a small private jet with a sleek, sophisticated interior. A cluster of four leather captain's chairs flank the center and Drake slides down into one near the window. Unsure of where to sit, I sit down in the chair across from him. The leather is inviting and supple under my fingers and

I relax just a little into the seat and take in my sur-roundings. Night has fallen quickly and it's almost completely dark outside. The interior of the jet is illuminated by little LED lights lining the pathway on the carpeting giving off a faint glow.

Drake lifts a glass decanter from a nearby table and pours a few measures of amber liquor into a crystal tumbler, then takes a long sip. He licks his full lower lip and closes his eyes, resting his head back against the plush leather seat.

There's no overhead announcement, no safety demonstration, and no warning. All of a sudden the jet's engines roar to life and we're barreling down the runway. I fumble with the buckle on my seatbelt, latching it just as we take flight. I can feel Drake's eyes on me, watching me curiously, but I don't dare lift my gaze.

When I finally look up, Drake's poured a glass of the alcohol for me and is holding it toward me. "It might help."

I'm not much of a drinker, and especially straight liquor, but I know he's right. I have no idea what he has planned for me, and this will probably be the only opportunity I have for pain manage-ment if I'm going to lose my virginity later.

He seems so calm and in control, it makes me wonder what might be lurking under the surface of that composed demeanor and expensive suit. A warm shiver races through me and I take a long sip of the drink, welcoming the burning path the liquor creates down my throat.

Colton

Tonight has been an absolute fucking debacle. One million dollars was more than I'd wanted to spend and more importantly, I didn't want a virgin. I'd wanted one of the older, more independent girls who'd done this type of thing before. Not someone I'd have to handhold and train every step of the way. Something tells me Sophie is going to take more time and work than I've bargained for.

I release a heavy sigh, and take a long swallow of bourbon, letting it warm a path down my throat. The dull roar of the jet engine is giving me a headache and I pour another measure into my glass.

Fuck's sake, what had I been thinking?

I glance over at the girl, she's finished her drink, and the way she's huddled into the leather chair—her knees pulled up to her chest, and her arms wrapped tightly around them—creams of her discomfort. Her eyes are closed as though she's trying to summon her inner strength for whatever is about to come her way. I can already tell this isn't going to go well. *Fuck.*

I'd only outbid that asshole who wanted her because he'd gotten the girl I had picked out. She was closer to my own age of twenty eight, and this was her third time entering into this type of relationship. She was tried and tested and would have made a good drama-free companion. But that prick had been the one to take her home, so when he started bidding on Sophie, outbidding him was my way of giving the asshole a taste of his own medicine. Plus, he just seemed like a dirt-bag and I didn't want him to have her. The little boy inside me wanted to take his toy and go home. Of course, the terrified, timid girl sitting across from me is now mine to deal with, so maybe I hadn't exactly thought that plan through.

And a virgin too…would she even be capable of handling me? I hadn't wanted a project—someone to babysit and go slow with. But shit, I'm the one in control. There's no real reason to go slow. I can set the pace of this. And I will.

As I continue studying her, my cock perks up in interest. She's petite, but with all the rounded curves a woman's body should have. Soft moldable tits and an ass meant for grabbing onto. Or spanking. Her skin is creamy and pale, except for the apples of her cheeks which are flushed pink. Long dark hair hangs loose over one shoulder. My gaze travels north and I realize her blue eyes have lifted to mine. She's watching me expectantly, obviously wondering what will happen next. Good fucking question.

I have no idea why I told her to call me Drake. Actually, I do. It doesn't take a psychologist to figure out that my employees call me Mr. Drake and hearing her call me Colton would feel too familiar. Too intimate. That isn't what this connection is about. It's business. Pure and simple. The business of my dick getting some much overdue attention and having a steady female companion without the hassle of navigating the dating scene. *Get your head in the fucking game, Colt.*

Sophie

The plane safely touches down after only about

thirty minutes or so, and once again, we climb on Drake's motorcycle, which I learn has been stored in the bulk luggage compartment underneath the plane. Darkness has fallen all around us, which fits my slightly buzzed and melancholy mood. I want to hide in the night shadows and pretend that none of this is real.

While I hold on to him for dear life, he expertly navigates us down the highway, the single headlight illuminating our path. I pay close attention to the passing signs. Apparently, we're near Los Angeles—a place I've never been. Soon he takes an exit for Malibu and once we're on the surface streets, my heart begins pounding. We're nearing our destination and I have no idea what's in store for me.

When we pull up to the gated drive, Drake stops the bike to punch some buttons on the key pad, and I peer around his shoulder, eager for a look at what will be my new home for the next six months. It can't really be described as a home…it's a full on mansion, complete with a stone drive leading up to a sprawling estate.

Little twinkling lights illuminate our path and provide me with just enough light to make my jaw drop open at what I can see. The house is stucco in the color of warm honey and two huge columns flank the rich mahogany front door. Drake cruises right on past the front of the house and parks beside a six-stall garage before cutting the ignition.

Here we go.

Butterflies take flight in my belly as he leads me toward the house. We navigate a winding stone path lit with landscape lighting toward a side entrance. I suppose it makes sense we aren't going all the way around to the massive front doors. That entrance is probably only used for guests, yet it's too strange to think that I live here now, that I'm not just a visiting guest.

I wonder if he's just going to leave his bike parked outside all night, but then realize he probably has someone on staff to pull it into the garage. I can't imagine he'd have a home this large and not have people hired to help him take care of it. I doubt he personally dusts the knick-knacks in the one hundred rooms, or however many this monstrosity has.

We enter through the glass-covered side door into what appears to be the world's finest mudroom. Tall pale wood lockers reach from floor to ceiling, a wire basket of umbrellas, a large tufted bench with a few throw pillows artfully arranged and a large area rug to cover the marble floors.

He tosses his suit coat and the helmets onto the bench and continues toward the hall. My eyes scan everything as I trail behind him.

"Front entry," he says, pointing to the darkened foyer that's even more impressive than I imagined. Dual winding staircases meet at the base of the foyer where there's a round table sporting a huge vase of pink peony blossoms. They smell incredible. Like sunshine and happiness. It seems like a girly touch, but I shrug off the thought. Again, I'm sure it wasn't chosen by him. Then again, I can't imagine anything in his world that he doesn't exercise complete control over.

"Formal living room," he points to the left, not even bothering to turn on a light or enter the room he's indicated. It looks cavernous and anything but welcoming with stiff, modern furniture. I struggle to take in every detail as he continues moving.

I realize he's giving me a tour, but it's rushed and impersonal. For someone who owns such a spectacular mansion, it seems like he'd take a little more pride in showing it off. Something seems off, but I can't put my finger on what.

He points out several more rooms, a cold dining room with a humongous table, a darkened library filled with books I get the sense he doesn't care about, and rarely bothers to read. "It's a beautiful library," I murmur. I long to run my fingertips along the dusty spines and go hunting for a treasure to read.

A look of dark emotion flashes in his eyes before he blinks it away, his carefully composed mask safely returning, before leading me away.

"Your home is lovely." My voice sounds hollow and stiff. Drake doesn't respond so I continue following him through the dimly lit maze of hallways.

My throat feels tight and I work to keep up with him.

"Where do you spend your time?"

My question stops him in his tracks and he turns to face me, his eyes focused on mine. He studies me for a moment as if trying to decide why I want this information. Call me crazy, but knowing a few details about the man I'm now living with and expected to service might be a teensy bit helpful, and so far this tour and his home have revealed nothing. He tips his head toward a far corridor. "This way."

Maybe I shouldn't have been so nosy, because

now as he leads me further into the belly of the house, all my fears rush to the surface. Does he have some weird sex room like Christian Grey's red room of pain?

He opens the door to a large office, complete with an executive style mahogany desk, black leather chair, charcoal gray sofa, and a mini bar built into the far wall. This room has a cozy feel to it with its rich wood furniture, plush carpeting and the subtle scent of his cologne that I smelled earlier. A set of glass doors lead out to a balcony. "Out here." He motions me forward as he crosses the room.

He opens the glass door and steps out onto a large deck overlooking the Pacific Ocean and I am stunned into speechlessness. The soft whoosh of waves in the background and the gentle breeze blowing my hair back from my face are immediately calming.

I can see why the opulent rooms of the house don't interest him. This is like a private oasis out here. Two wooden lounge chairs outfitted with comfy looking cushions and a small round table nestled between them are the only pieces of furniture, but it's perfect. Anything more would clutter the space.

He lets me take in the peaceful setting, and when he breaks the silence a moment later, it temporarily startles me. "You'll probably discover I work too much." He points toward the office. "And I come out here to unwind."

I nod in silent acknowledgment. It might not be much, but he's exposed a small piece of himself, and I tuck the knowledge away. He's a workaholic and perhaps a contemplative man, spending his time alone with the sounds of the water to keep him company.

We head back inside and Drake completes the tour—there's an outdoor swimming pool and garden that I only peek at through the window, as well as a home gym one level down.

Finally he leads me into a den with huge windows that overlook the ocean and has a sectional couch and large flat screen TV mounted above a fireplace.

"This is it," he says, voice somewhat serious.

All this just for him? It must get lonely.

He stands in silence studying me for what feels like too long. Realizing that the tour is over, my eyes fall to the floor. Are we going to have sex now? Here in the den? I imagined it'd be in his bedroom, but I suppose this is better than a weird sex dungeon or some other strange alternative. I have no idea what his interests and preferences are, but I suppose I'm about to learn. My heart thuds dully in my chest.

"Eyes up," he orders again.

There's something he dislikes about my refusal to meet his eyes. Is he ashamed he bought me? It's as though he wants to pretend all this is normal. I'll play along. For now. I don't know what he is capable of, and I don't want to anger him. I meet his gaze. What I see is an intense man—his dark eyes speak of pain and past trauma, and someone fighting to practice restraint, if the tick in his jaw is any evidence.

"You don't have to be so skittish around me. I'm not going to hurt you, sweetness."

I draw a fortifying breath. I want to believe him. His tone is sincere, as is the nickname, and the way he's gazing over at me feels non-threatening, but still, all my senses are on high alert. I need to keep myself on guard until I have my bearings.

"Come sit down." He crosses the room and sits in the center of the large gray sectional sofa.

I sit down in the spot next to him, my breathing erratic. I should thank him for the money but I don't know his intentions. "I'm sorry. I'm just new to this whole sex slave thing," I say instead.

He runs one hand through his hair, looking deep in thought. "Yeah, me too."

"I'm your first?"

"Something like that." He grins at me and my belly flips. He really is an attractive man.

"I'm not sure how it works…or what to expect," I admit.

"Would it put you at ease if I explained some things to you?"

I nod, and fold my hands in my lap. A lesson—perfect.

"I'm a busy man, Sophie. I run two companies and have little time to pursue extra- curricular activities. You're here to satisfy my physical cravings—to take care of my needs. I will satisfy your financial needs. Half of the money is being transferred into your account tonight and as long as you remain with me and comply to the contract, you will receive the remaining balance at the end of the six months. Your discretion is very important to me. I know you've signed a non-disclosure agreement, but I need your word that you'll tell no one about our arrangement." His eyes lift to mine. "Not even your best friend. No one."

The thought of telling Becca the truth about what I've done never even crossed my mind. "I won't. I don't want anyone knowing about this either." I knew I'd need to explain the money somehow, but I figured I could tell my family it was from an anonymous donor at the hospital. The first installment—five hundred thousand, minus what I owed Bill, will be in my account tomorrow. It's more than enough to pay for Becca's treatment. The fleeting idea of ditching him once I have the money crosses through my brain. But realizing there'll be no way I could ever pay him back, I know I need to fulfill my end of the contract.

"Good. We'll need to craft a story for the public, friends and families about why you're here, but as long as you prove to be trustworthy, there's no reason I can't give you some of the freedoms of a normal life. In the meantime, you're free to use the house as your own, the pool, gardens, and gym are all open to you."

I nod again. I wonder if I'd be free to leave the premises and go for a jog, but for now I keep my lips sealed. I don't want to push my luck the first night. Besides, if he is the vindictive type, once he knows that's important to me, he could hold it over my head as punishment. I look up at the giant television screen in front of us and wonder what he intends for the rest of the night.

"What do you want?" I murmur, gathering my courage. It's better to know what's coming at me, so I have a chance to mentally prepare.

His eyes wander over to mine and he smirks. "I want what all men want when they spend a cool mil for a virgin."

Oh god. It's happening tonight. I hadn't even had time to prepare. I'm still tender from my waxing. I wonder if he'll give me an extra day or two if I tell him.

"I want a cold beer and to watch the sports highlights," he finishes.

All the air rushes from my lungs in a whoosh. "That's all?"

Still watching my reaction, he lifts one dark brow. "Honestly, I'd love a blowjob, but considering the mistrust in your eyes, I'm not sure having your teeth that close to my dick would be the wisest decision."

"I wouldn't…"

"You wouldn't what? Blow me? That's part of the agreement, sweetness, and if you tell me you don't like sucking cock, we're going to have a problem." His voice is deep, rich, and sends a flash of heat over my skin.

"No, I meant I wouldn't bite you." I'm not a violent person.

He smiles at me, his full lips parting to reveal straight white teeth. Apparently that news has made him happy. He looks friendly and relaxed when he smiles at me like that and I imagine him being a regular guy, someone I'd meet out at a bar and flirt with. I'd let him buy me a drink and fantasize about kissing those soft lips as we spoke. Blinking several times, I realize I've been watching his mouth for too long and my eyes dart back up to his.

His smile fades and his hands go to his belt buckle, unlatching the silver clasp with a soft click and sliding it free. Seeing the thick leather belt in his hands makes me nervous. I don't know his sexual tastes. Will he want to restrain and whip me? But he drops the belt to the floor and pops open the button on his pants, then slides down the zipper, all the while keeping those intense blue eyes on mine.

My heart hammers in my chest. *Holy shit.* This is really going to happen. I'm going to give a blow-job to a complete stranger.

"On your knees." His voice is rough and filled with an edge of desire.

With my pulse thrumming wildly at the base of my throat, my body obeys his command, moving from the couch to the floor to kneel between his feet. Having removed his shoes, I notice his feet are long and narrow and encased in black silk socks.

Pushing his dress pants down his hips, his hand disappears under the fabric of his black boxer briefs. His stormy blue eyes hold mine while he strokes the growing bulge, as he seems to word-lessly inquire if this is okay.

What choice do I have? I can't have him return-ing me. I give him an imperceptible nod. And god, the truth is, I'm curious. What is wrong with me that I want to know if his cock is as glorious as the rest of him?

Placing one palm against my cheek, he guides me closer and bends his head to mine, letting our lips touch just briefly. The gesture is unexpected-ly tender. I draw a shuddering breath and part my lips, wetting them with my tongue and he presses forward again, tasting the moisture I've left on my bottom lip. His lips are soft and generous, and he pulls my bottom lip slightly into his mouth and sucks gently before sliding his tongue against mine.

Oh wow.

His kiss is cautious and slow, like he's testing me, checking for my reaction. I remain still, letting him explore, and carefully return his kiss, my tongue reaching out to lick against his.

I'd be lying if I said having his hot mouth on mine didn't affect me. I'm warm and flustered knowing his hand remains tucked inside his boxers stroking himself while his tongue strokes mine. My entire body feels alive with energy.

Just when I'm ready for more he breaks away from the kiss, leaving my lips damp and swollen. The hand cupping my cheek moves to pull his boxers down and he lifts his cock free from the material, letting it rest against his belly. I venture a glance down.

Sacred mother of everything holy, that is one giant cock.

It reaches up toward his belly button, and is incredibly thick too. I can't possibly be expected to fit that in my mouth. Suddenly his fears about me biting him seem a very real possibility. I'll need to unhinge my jaw to accommodate that thing. He remains still, letting me take my fill. I open my mouth to protest, but his hand moves to the back of my neck, guiding me closer.

"Come here, Sophie," he breathes my name, the sound of it on his lips both foreign and enticing. The warm weight of his palm on my nape sends little fractures of heat spiraling down the back of my neck and spine. Still holding me close, he adjusts himself, freeing his balls from the briefs next so all of him is exposed. They are large, round and smooth. Everything about him is so intensely male and perfect, it's hard not to react. My body pulses with electric heat, as feelings I never imagined I'd have course through me. Interest. Desire. Lust.

He's attractive, fit and intelligent. There's nothing about him, at least physically, not to like, but he *bought* me for heaven's sake. I should feel repulsed, not excited and slightly turned on. But I guess I can't control my primal reactions.

He watches me expectantly and I lift his heavy cock away from where it rests against his tight abdominal muscles and lower my head to his lap, my tongue darting out to taste the tip of him. He releases a small grunt of satisfaction and tightens his grip against the back of my neck, urging me closer.

Curling my fist around the base of him, I work my tongue up and down his length, coating him in my saliva so my hand can easily slide up and down. I'll never be able to fit all of him in my mouth, so using my hands too is a necessity.

A softly murmured curse urges me on. My free hand reaches beneath to gently cup and massage his balls. A warm drop of fluid escapes him and I swipe my tongue against his tip, capturing the bead of salty fluid and swallow it down. Another murmured grunt urges me on.

Keeping up my suction around the head of his cock, I ease open my jaw, trying to fit as much of him as I can into my mouth. While my mouth takes him in, I use both hands to firmly stroke the neglected half of his generous length.

"Oh fuck," Drake growls. Warmth and moisture flood my panties and I commit myself fully, sucking, licking and stroking to the best of my ability. "That's it, just like that," his deep voice rumbles in his chest.

Confusion snaps to the forefront of my brain. No part of me should be enjoying this, but I feel powerful and desirable making this gorgeous man come apart.

His hand tightens in my hair, causing my scalp to tingle and he pulls my mouth away, taking his enormous cock in his hand and stroking it in short, uneven strokes. My core clenches at the sight of him.

"Open your mouth," he moans. I do as I'm told, opening wide for him. "Let me see your tongue." I stick out my tongue and he places the head of his cock against it as his fist continues pumping. His eyes fall closed and his head drops back against the sofa. "Oh fuck, sweetness," he growls as a low rumble vibrates in his chest. "That feels so fucking good." Watching us once again, he keeps stroking himself, his pace erratic and his eyes dark with lust. "Your mouth looks so pretty on my cock."

I fight the urge to close my mouth around him and suck, but instead remain kneeling before him, my mouth open, waiting to catch his come. Seconds later, warm drops of semen spurt onto my outstretched tongue.

He watches as the last of his release lands in my waiting mouth. His eyes are filled with desire and appreciation. I swallow and sit back on my heels while he tucks himself back into his pants and pulls up the zipper. "I'd say you passed your first test."

His tone is one of pleasant surprise.

Some strange part of me feels proud. I tell myself it was only because I want to make sure he doesn't return me and request a refund. But our shared erotic experience has left me shaken and feeling vulnerable. There's no denying that a part of me enjoyed that—enjoyed his fist tightening in my hair and hearing him voice his pleasure when he climaxed. And my damp panties and pounding heart signal that I'm not ready for the night to be over. Feelings of shame slam against me. I shouldn't have enjoyed any part of that. *God, what is wrong with me?*

Drake rises from the couch and strides from the room without a backward glance, leaving me sitting alone on the carpeting.

Several moments later I hear sounds coming from a nearby room and since I know it's just me and him in the house, I go to investigate.

I find him in the kitchen, a bottle of beer lifted to his lips and the thick column of his throat moving as he swallows long gulps of the icy liquid.

The kitchen is immaculate. My eyes wander from the elegant white and grey marbled countertops to the rich wood cabinets to the state of the art stainless steel appliances gleaming all shiny and new. A large basket sits atop the island overflowing with baguettes, heads of garlic, lemons and what I assume are pomegranates. I wonder if he likes to cook.

"You want anything to eat?" he asks, lowering the bottle, but still not turning to face me.

"No thanks." I haven't eaten, but food is the last thing on my mind. "Maybe just some water," I answer.

He shoots me a knowing grin and my cheeks heat. Yes, I need to wash the taste of his semen from my mouth and apparently we are both thinking it. He grabs a bottle of water from the large commercial grade double door stainless steel refrigerator and twists off the cap before handing it to me.

"Thanks," I murmur, taking a long sip. I feel the cool water sink to the bottom of my empty belly. It's refreshing and crisp. My first bit of peace since this whole evening started. I drain half of the bottle while gazing around the kitchen.

I spot a block of knives near the eight-burner gas stove and an errant thought passes through my brain. *I could hurt him and escape.* But why would I do that? He's given me exactly what I wanted.

Instead I finish my water in silence while he continues to watch me curiously.

Colton

This wasn't a first date—there wasn't an order to adhere to. There was no need to round first base and kiss her like that before she sucked my cock. She is mine to do with what I please. I could have fucked her in the ass on the kitchen table if I'd wanted. And believe me, the thought crossed my mind. When I'd watched her bend over my bike and set the helmet on the seat, I wanted to bite into her ass like an apple. Then take her plump cheeks into my hands and drive forward into the center of them, maybe smack her ass too for making me have such depraved thoughts. Instead I'd acted like a concerned boyfriend, kissing her lips and making sure she was in the right frame of mind before using her for my pleasure. And fuck, her mouth had been perfect. Warm and soft and eager to please. I guess knowing someone had just paid a small fortune for your company ensured good service.

Coming on her tongue wasn't enough. After, I'd wanted to strip her naked and fuck her hard, ending by jerking off on her tits to mark her and show her she was mine. But there'll be time for that later.

In the meantime, I want to know her story. She seems like a nice, normal girl—too nice for the sick shit I'm pulling her into. But her reasons for being here aren't my concern. Just like my reasons for obtaining her aren't any of hers. She doesn't need to know my past, the only things she needs to know are that I like my cock sucked regularly, I have a healthy appetite for sex and not to disturb me when I'm working. And I need to remember she's here for one purpose. If so, this arrangement will work out fine, and leave us both satisfied.

"Let's go to bed, tomorrow will be a long day and you'll need your rest."

Her skittish blue eyes dart to mine again and she nods tentatively. She wants to know when I'm going to fuck her. I guess she'll have to wait and see.

CHAPTER THREE

Sophie

O nce upstairs we pass by several doors and continue on down the long hall. When we reach the master bedroom, I grow quiet, taking it all in. The room is huge, with a king sized bed and an upholstered headboard, tables with lamps, and a chaise lounge chair in front of a gas fireplace. The décor is contemporary and simple in tones of light gray and cream with splashes of blue as accents. Everything looks brand new.

"Master bath." He points off to the side of the bedroom suite.

His one word responses and grunts ever since I'd pleasured him are grating on my nerves. Why is he acting so detached and strange? "I'm sorry if

I've done something wrong…" I start.

Drake's eyes lift to mine. "Get undressed, Sophie."

A gasp of breath sticks in my throat. "What?"

"You heard me." His deep voice sends a ripple of anticipation through me.

This is it.

We're standing in the center of his bedroom with all the lights on. And his dark eyes are hungry and roaming over me. Even though I'm still fully clothed, I've never felt more exposed. His intense gaze holds the power to make me feel vulnerable and bare like no one has before.

With trembling hands, I unbutton my jeans and slide them down my legs, letting them puddle to the floor at my ankles, where I kick them off and toe them aside. I forget trying to be sexy. I've never given a sexy strip tease in my life, and I have a feeling if I try to start now, I'll only look like a foolish little girl. Next I lift my shirt over my head and remove it, depositing it with the jeans. I try to suck in my stomach and stand taller to best show off my assets. God, I feel like a piece of art work on display. And worse, why am I so desperate for this man's approval?

"Don't," he says, his voice low.

I swallow and release the breath I've been holding, my shoulders relaxing and my body returning to its natural state. I stare straight ahead, meeting his eyes, unflinching, and not daring to look away. Something inside me feels rebellious and strong, even though I'm obviously the one in the weaker position right now.

"Take off your bra," he says next, his voice a rough growl.

My fingers reach behind my back and I release the clasp, my heart thundering against my ribcage as I let the bra fall away. My instinct is to cover my breasts yet again, shield myself from his view, but deciding it would be pointless and show how weak and helpless I feel, I let the bra drop to the floor between us. My nipples tighten in the cool night air, begging for attention. I've been wound tight ever since I'd sucked his cock, my panties slightly damp and my body aching and confused. I shouldn't want this — I shouldn't crave this moment between us, but knowing we've been building toward it all night only makes me want to see it through.

"The panties too, sweetness," he whispers roughly, his voice sending little darts of electricity flickering across my skin.

Sucking in a deep breath, I push my fingers into my panties, easing them down my hips and giving my bottom a little wiggle as they round my backside and drift to the floor.

His eyes are still locked on mine. He hasn't looked down at my now completely naked body and something about his control unsettles me. I felt no such restraint when it came to perusing his body. My eyes had greedily soaked in every detail.

I never expected to be physically attracted to the man who purchased me, and I know it will only complicate things for me. It's disheartening knowing I don't have the same effect on him. Maybe he's not impressed.

But finally, his eyes begin a slow descent, wandering down my body like we have all the time in the world, and his tongue wanders out to meet his bottom lip.

His gaze settles on my breasts. They feel so full and heavy they're practically throbbing. *Does he want me?* I'm not sure why that matters to me, but suddenly I know that it does. My self-esteem has never been entirely robust, but it's never been completely lacking either. Yet there's something about standing nude before a rich, powerful, sinfully attractive man that makes me want to measure up.

Drake swallows, the bulge in his throat bobbing, before lowering his eyes to my bare juncture between my thighs. I want to press my legs together, but I remain steady. Heat zips through me as his gaze rises, glancing up to meet my eyes again. That's it? He ordered me to strip just to look at me?

But then my gaze lowers and I see the long, thick erection rising in his pants. The only indication that he likes what he sees. *Then why won't you do something about it?* The errant thought flashes through my brain, along with a catalog of erotic images—his full mouth at my throat, the feel of his large palms cupping my breasts as his thumbs move over the sensitive peaks. I would grip his solid arms, lay my head against his warm chest and come undone as his cock, that I know from experience is hot and hard, nudges restlessly at my center. A warm shiver races up my spine and I swallow down a helpless whimper.

"What do you like to sleep in?" he asks, his voice completely composed and unshaken.

"Usually a t-shirt and pajama pants," I say, digging my big toe into the plush carpeting.

He nods and heads for the closet, retrieving a gray t-shirt and a pair of cotton pants for me. They're both a size large—but they're soft and comfortable as I slide them over my overheated skin. I ball my discarded clothes into a pile and wonder where I'm supposed to put them. I have nothing here, no belongings, no sense of purpose and the realization is dizzying. I shouldn't have been focused on tempting him with my curves. I needed to be clear-headed and figuring out how to survive in my new life.

Drake enters the bathroom and closes the door behind him, giving me a chance to wander the large suite uninterrupted. I pad across the floor toward the closet and realize that I've never felt carpeting so thick and soft before. It's like it's padded underneath with pillows of cotton. It's heavenly. A slight smile curls on my lips. At least I'm able to find some silver lining in this crazy situation. I live in a freaking mansion. And besides, it could be a lot worse.

As I wander toward the closet, I can't help but notice the faint scent of women's perfume that clings to the interior of the bedroom. The scent is stale, but it's still present. Lingering like a mystery. I wonder briefly who the perfume belonged to.

The large walk-in closet is bigger than my bedroom back home. One half is filled with designer suits in various shades of black, navy, gray and pinstripes, a rolodex of ties in every color hangs from one wall, neatly folded stacks of cotton shirts rest on built-in shelves along with various men's items. A stray watch, a leather portfolio, cuff links, loose change. But the main thing that stands out to me is that one entire half of the closet has been emptied out — just a few loose padded hangers remain along with a red silk camisole dangling from one of them haphazardly.

I wonder what happened to the owner of the perfume and the camisole. He said I was his first sex slave, so perhaps she was an ex-girlfriend. My brain fills in the details, giving him the benefit of the doubt too much, I'm sure, but I imagine his failed romantic relationship is due to his vigorous work schedule and his closed off nature. Enter his need for someone like me. Regular sex without the commitment of an actual relationship. I push the useless theories from my head, knowing they won't do me any good. I'm stuck here with him, regardless of his background and issues, and I have to make the best of it.

A big part of me wants to believe he's a nice, normal guy who's been through something tragic that pushed him into hiring a sex slave, but the truth is, I have no idea. He could be a crazed psycho with a penchant for too rough sex and kink I've never even imagined. *Yay, me.*

I stuff my wadded up clothes into an empty basket on the shelf of the closet and return to the bedroom. I grab my phone from my purse and sit down on the bed.

I send a quick text to my mom, and then Becca letting them both know I've decided to visit a friend in LA and will be out of town for a while. I know it's low—letting them know through text message that I am essentially a runaway, but I hope they'll understand. There's too much pressure at home. Taking a spur of the minute vacation isn't outside the realm of possibility. In fact, they'll both probably be happy.

Becca's text back is a smiley face, followed by a note that I should have a hot fling with a surfer and then tell her all the gory details. My mom's return text simply asks when I'll be home and I responded honestly— hat I don't know, but probably not for a while. It scares me to think about what could happen to Becca in the time I'm away. In the morning, I'll let her know about the money.

The bathroom door opens and Drake is standing there expectantly. He's dressed in just his black boxer shorts I got a peek at earlier and his body still has the ability to make my jaw unhinge, but I'm more prepared for it this time. I keep my expression neutral, even though I've never seen such sculpted pecs and an eight-pack outside of men's fitness magazines. He is positively lickable.

I stuff my phone back in my purse and rise from the bed. I'm curious about the sleeping arrangements he's envisioned. We're in his master bedroom...so does that mean?

He pulls back the soft-looking white puffy down comforter and folds back the sheet. "Companionship is part of the deal for me. I don't like sleeping alone," he says, as if reading my thoughts.

So the big bad CEO is afraid of the dark? A small part of me feels comforted by this fact — it makes him more human somehow. The bed is plenty big enough to accommodate us both and if I'd been locked in a room of my own all night, I would crumble into a sobbing hysterical mess as the gravity of my new living situation hit me. Being near him means I have to keep my carefully crafted mask in place. Besides, I'm used to sharing a bedroom with Becca since we were infants, and the idea of sleeping alone in an unfamiliar place doesn't appeal to me. I was sure the sounds and groans from the house would keep me up most of the night, my mind churning. At least I'll have someone nearby if something happened. Of course this same someone could roll toward me in the night expecting sex. But something tells me the sex won't happen tonight. I have to take my chances, not that I have a choice, I remind myself. I am his to do with what he pleases.

I crawl into the far side of the bed and curl into a tight ball, praying for sleep to come easy.

"No fuckin' way," he grunts. "Over here, sweetness."

I exhale slowly and slide my body closer to his, keeping my back to him, only stopping when the firm wall of male warmth stops me. He wraps one heavy arm around my middle and tugs me close, until my back is pressed against his chest. My heart kicks up speed in my chest. There's something about this close, intimate contact that unravels me. Although I'm used to sharing a bedroom with Becca, I'm certainly not accustomed to spooning with a man all night long. Let alone one I hardly know who's already turned me into a puddle of hormones. *Geez.*

His rough hand settles against my bare hip and

my breathing instantly falters. His fingers splay open across my abdomen, lightly caressing me. My muscles stiffen as I wait for his hand to push between my legs, taking what I've kept guarded most of my life.

"Relax," he encourages, his voice whispery soft and sleepy. "Nothing more will happen tonight." He continues rubbing me—my hip, the indent of my belly, the top of my thigh, almost like he's testing me, training me to be comfortable with him. The warmth of his breath against my hair and his hand lightly caressing my skin make it tough to relax, but eventually I do, growing accustomed to the new sensations. My eyes slip closed and I enjoy the soothing touch he's delivering before drifting off to sleep.

CHAPTER FOUR

Sophie

I'm not sure what I expected, but the following morning when I roll over in the gigantic bed, Drake is already gone. The crinkled white Egyptian cotton sheets are the only bit of evidence he'd been there at all. He was a good sleeping companion. Quiet and true to his word, he didn't try anything with me.

I stretch leisurely and take my time rolling from the bed. In the opulent bathroom, I debate taking a shower—I'm dying to use the luxurious steam shower with its six shower heads, but decide instead to make it brief in case Drake is expecting me downstairs.

After smoothing my hair down in the mirror, I wander downstairs in search of coffee. The house

y

FILTHY *beautiful* LIES | 59

is completely silent. As I pass by room after room on my way to the kitchen, it feels like I'm walking through a museum.

Drake is sitting at the breakfast bar, leaning over his iPad with a cup of steaming espresso sitting nearby.

"Morning," I say.

His gaze lifts up to meet mine, his mouth tugged down in a frown. I feel like I'm interrupting him. He taps a few more keys on his tablet and then glances up again, his frown now absent. "Morning."

"Is there coffee?" He said I should make myself at home, and so I try to fight off the feeling that I should retreat to a dark corner of the house and stop interrupting him.

He tips his head to the elaborate stainless steel brewing system installed into one wall. That is not a coffee pot. It could very well be a time machine for all I know. "My staff—the housekeepers and cook have all been made aware of your presence here. They think you're a friend who's staying with me. So if you need anything, don't hesitate to ask. Marta's my favorite. You can trust her, okay?"

I nod. "So, what's our story? About how I know

you."

A crease permeates his brow as he thinks it over. "You're the younger sister of a college friend of mine. You're in LA trying to make it as a model and I offered you a place to stay until you get a job. How does that sound?"

"A model?" Me? I glance down at myself and nearly roll my eyes. I don't have the height or weight requirements to be a model. "Let's make our story at least somewhat believable."

"Yes. A model. And it is believable."

I chew on my lower lip, internalizing this information at how he views me. "Okay." *Whatever.* "Does this brother of mine have a name?"

He thinks it over. "Anthony."

"I'm not Italian."

"Fine, John."

"Where did you and John go to college?"

"Harvard," he says without batting an eyelash.

Wow. Impressive. I guess the multi-million dollar home sitting directly on the beach in Malibu and the running two companies thing makes sense. He has a top notch education. He's smart, powerful, and sexy. Altogether, a lethal combination. I still don't understand how he's single. "Are you from the east coast originally?" I ask.

He nods. "Connecticut."

Just then, the doorbell rings—it's an obnoxious chime that goes on for what seems like forever. My eyes flick over to his. "Are you expecting someone?"

He sets the porcelain espresso cup down on the counter. "I guess it's a good thing we came up with that story," he says, then heads off to answer the door.

What the hell? I'm standing in his kitchen wearing the baggy T-shirt he gave me last night, no bra, and paper thin cotton pants without any panties, and apparently I'm about to meet someone from his life. *Perfect.*

Seconds later, Drake reenters the kitchen, flanked by two men who share his same features. The resemblance is uncanny. My first thought is: *there are three of him?*

It's overwhelming to have them all in the same room, all of their brilliant blue eyes watching me.

"Who's this?" One of the Drake look-alikes

asks with a cocky grin. His eyes are devouring me and his mouth is curved up in a crooked smile. He looks to be a few years younger than Drake, which makes me realize for the first time that Drake must have a couple of years on me.

"Sophie, these are my brothers." He points to the cocky-grinned younger version of himself. "Pace." And then to the slightly taller version with kind eyes, "And Collins."

"Hello." I tug at the hem of the t-shirt I'm wearing, all too aware of my braless state. Shit, and I'm sure my hair's a wicked wreck too. "It's nice to meet you."

"Last night's conquest is still here?" Pace's mouth tugs up in another of those uneven grins I'm already coming to love.

"Sophie is John's youngest sister."

"John?" They both ask in unison.

Here we go. Time to test the story.

"John—from Harvard. He was one of Derek's buddies."

Both brothers nod like this makes perfect sense. I suppose there are a lot of Johns at Harvard, and since they have no reason to doubt him, they quickly accept the story. I breathe a little sigh of relief while Drake finishes explaining that I've just moved to LA and I'm looking for a modeling job, so he offered me a place to stay since he has like fifteen empty bedrooms.

"Where are you from originally?" Collins asks.

"Boston," I blurt without thinking. That's where Harvard is, but I wince realizing I'm completely missing the telltale Boston accent. *Nice, Sophie.*

"So you guys aren't, like, an item, then?" Pace presses on. He eyes my ensemble—it's obvious I've slept in Drake's clothes.

"No," Drake answers without offering anything further.

"The airline lost my luggage," I explain, gesturing to my outfit.

"Bastards." Pace grins at me again.

"I'm Collins. It's good to meet you." The eldest of the three extends his hand to mine and gives it a warm shake, his large hand completely enclosing my own palm. His blue eyes crinkle in the corners and seem to see too much. It's the same feeling I get looking directly into Drake's eyes.

"You too."

"Ignore these two idiots. Welcome to the City of Angeles. If you need anything, please let me know," he says.

"Isn't Tatianna a model, bro?" Pace looks at Collins and asks.

"Who?" Collins' eyes still haven't wandered from mine.

"Your girlfriend," Pace reminds him. "Your very committed, live-in girlfriend."

Drake almost chokes on his laughter.

"Right. Yes, that's what I meant." Collins straightens his shoulders. "If you need anything while you're here and trying to get established, let me know, and I'll see if I can help."

Pace and Drake are both chuckling at their older brother. Watching them interact, I can see they're a close-knit family and I immediately miss Becca. Although it's been a while since she and I could just have fun and joke around so carefree like this. Lately there's been too many hospitals, too much stress, and too many bills to even remember how to laugh, let alone breathe.

"Thank you, I will let you know." I tip my head to the floor. My desire for coffee is gone, all I want to do is flee this kitchen and these three big men who are all watching me closely. I want to take a shower, put on a damn bra and get dressed.

"What the fuck, Coco, don't you have anything of Stella's she could put on until the airline finds her luggage?" Pace questions, throwing a mock punch toward Drake.

The glare Drake shoots him is akin to an atomic bomb going off in the kitchen. Note to self: Do not anger Drake, or Coco... or whatever his name is.

Whoever she is, Drake's body language screams that the name Stella should not be mentioned in his presence. Of course, this only makes me more curious.

"I'll call Marta," Drake says, rather than answering the direct question.

"On her one day off?" Collins raises an eyebrow.

I watch their exchange in fascination, I get the sense there is so much not being said that I need a translator just to keep up.

Drake turns to face me, his expression softening. "Go upstairs and shower if you like. I can give you fresh clothes to change into until Marta can get here. I forgot that I have plans to go golfing with my brothers today. But she'll take you shopping and get you everything you need. Until your luggage arrives," he adds, giving me a smirk.

"Okay," I mumble. I hate feeling so helpless, but I can do nothing but depend on him, my new, confusing master. Before retreating up the stairs, I give both brothers another handshake and we exchange goodbyes. Then I duck off to the safety of the master suite, needing a few minutes alone to recover from all the testosterone taking up residence in the kitchen.

CHAPTER FIVE

Sophie

O nce I'm alone upstairs, I know I can't delay the phone call I need to make any longer. I sit down on the upholstered chaise lounge chair in the master suite and dial my mom's cell, waiting anxiously for her to pick up.

"Sophie?"

"Yeah, it's me, Mom." With all that's happened in the past twenty-four hours, it's more grounding than I realized just to hear her voice.

"Where are you?" she asks.

"In LA, staying with a friend. I needed some time away—a break."

She's quiet and I know she's processing what I've told her. I don't have any friends in Los Angeles, but she doesn't question me.

"This friend I'm staying with…he, he owns a company and he's graciously offered to um," I stumble over my words, drawing a deep breath. God, I suck at lying. "He's offered to front the money to get Becca into the trial program."

"What have you done, Sophie?" her tone desperate and more harsh than I recall.

It's not the reaction I'm expecting.

"The money is in your account. Use it to get Becca the care she needs." My voice is almost clinical as I fight to hold my emotions together. Never once in my wildest imagination had I thought my mom would be suspicious of me. Of course I knew she'd wonder where the money came from, but I thought she'd be so grateful that she'd accept the story of a generous anonymous donor without argument.

She doesn't say anything else about the money, but I hear her sniffle. "How long will you be away?"

"A while," I confirm.

"Take care of yourself."

"I will. Just take care of Becca. I love you

guys."

"Sophie?" I hear Drake's voice from the hall before he steps into the room.

I toss my phone down onto the chair and stand, quickly wiping my cheeks with the back of my hands. "Yes?"

He's holding a coffee cup on a saucer and carrying a miniature pitcher of cream. "You didn't get your coffee."

The gesture is sweet and unexpected. I accept the cup from him, the fragrant brew is exactly what I need right now. There's a packet of sugar and a tiny stirring spoon on the saucer.

"I didn't know how you took it."

"With cream and sugar. This is perfect. Thank you."

He nods. "Everything…okay?"

"Yes." I straighten my spine. He didn't pay for drama and I'm sure he doesn't want to hear about my problems back home. "I just called my mom. Everything's going to be fine now." At least that's what I'm telling myself.

A frown line momentarily creases his forehead,

before his expression returns to the relaxed, neutral one I've come to expect. "Marta should be here in about an hour. You'll probably want to get yourself ready."

"Thanks again." I tip the coffee to my lips and watch as he exits the room.

After finishing my coffee, I decide to prepare for Marta's arrival. I run myself a bubble bath in the extra-large soaker tub and sink into the warmth, letting the hot water strip away my earlier tension.

The basket beside the tub is stocked with everything I could need and more — luxury bath salts, shampoo, conditioner, facial scrub, razors, and body washes in several different scents. I lose myself in the process, lathering my hair and skin and enjoying the peaceful moment and the fragrant scent of herbs enveloping me.

Until I hear the bathroom door open.

I squeak and dive for cover under the bubbles as Drake's lazy smile lights up his entire face and makes my belly flip.

"Nothing I haven't already seen, sweetness. Relax. I'm going to grab a shower. Do I need to use another bathroom, or are you cool with this?"

Hmm, let's see. Am I cool with the fact that I now live with a man who's seemingly comfortable sharing a bathroom with me while we're both naked as jaybirds? N-to-the-o. Privacy used to be something I valued. I merely nod.

He twists one of the nobs in the gigantic glass enclosed shower and water pours from the rain-like shower head mounted in the ceiling, then he tugs his shirt off over his head and steps out of the cotton pants he's wearing. I glimpse a firm, hard ass before slamming my eyes shut. Jesus…does he spend *all* his free time at the gym?

The urge to glance over at his nude, muscular body is driving me crazy. I can hear the water spraying against the stone shower floor and the sound is maddening. It's like being told there's a priceless oil painting hanging on the wall and you're prohibited from looking at it. Basically, it's torture. I already know what his manhood looks like, but the desire to steal a peak at the rest of him is almost overwhelming. I resist the temptation, but just barely.

I quickly finish my bath, thankful that I'd already washed up before Drake decided to join me. I secure the huge white fluffy towel around my body and exit the bathroom as quickly as I can, leaving a puddle of water on the floor in my wake.

Rather than dressing in my clothes from yesterday, I follow Drake's lead and put on the clothes he's laid out for me—another large t-shirt and sweat pants this time, comb out my hair. After, I venture downstairs for a refill on my coffee.

His brothers are both still in the kitchen and Pace is ransacking the fridge while Collins sits at the island, talking on his cell phone and looking perturbed.

"So, golfing today, huh?" I attempt to make small talk.

"You want to join us?" Pace asks.

I look down at my ensemble. "I don't think I'm dressed for it."

He chuckles. "True. But it'd give the stogy old men at Collins' country club something to talk about other than their stock performance."

I glance longingly over at the built in coffee machine and then down at my empty cup.

Pace's easy smile is back. God, that thing's becoming addictive. "C'mere, beautiful. Let me show you."

He takes the cup from me and sets it down on the tiny platform opening and shows me which buttons to press while muttering to himself about the damn pretentious machine. The options are overwhelming for a simple cup of coffee. I've never been good with gadgets and this is like a having a live-in barista. The LED display confirms my order—*small coffee* and I tap *brew* on the touch pad. I'm rewarded with the satisfying sound of the coffee beginning to pour into my cup and another one of Pace's adorable grins.

After adding a splash of milk and a bit of sugar into my coffee, I see Drake enter the kitchen. He's dressed smartly in dark grey khaki style pants and a white collared shirt that stretches across his muscled chest. Geez, they're like a polo team—or an advertisement for male cologne. You know, one of those where they're in white pants with bare feet sailing a yacht, smiling at you with gleaming, straight teeth. Drake's intense stare that I can feel deep inside me, coupled with Pace's lopsided smile is, overwhelming.

I set my coffee down on the island with shaking hands as Drake stalks toward me.

Colton

Approaching Sophie where she stands near the kitchen island, it's impossible to keep my eyes from slipping down over her lush curves. Her nipples have hardened against the t-shirt she's wearing. *My* t-shirt. I don't like that she's on display in front of my brothers. And Pace needs to keep his damn eyes to himself. If I see that dumbass dopey grin on his face one more time, I'm going to punch it off.

Looking at her, and imagining what's under that t-shirt, I struggle to keep my thoughts clean. My mind wanders back to last night when she stripped for me.

At the auction when she kept her arms locked over her breasts, I assumed there was something she was hiding. I didn't think it was anything as grotesque as a third nipple, but I'd thought maybe she had a birthmark, or a mole, or some other imperfection she wanted to keep hidden from the men bidding on her. But there was no such imperfection.

Sophie was fucking delicious. From her full,

heavy tits with small peach-colored nipples, to her long, toned legs to her bare pussy—which had been quite unexpected. My cock aches just thinking about it. She'd stripped herself bare for me last night. Her courage was almost overwhelming. She thought I was the one who held the power in our little exchange, but I was smart enough to know, without a doubt, it was her. My brave girl.

I stalk closer and her trembling hands place the cup and saucer on the counter, but her eyes remain on mine, just like I'd reminded her last night. I'm glad she doesn't cower from me, especially not in front of my brothers.

"Marta will take care of you today. She'll get you what you need, okay?"

She nods, her posture unsure. I hadn't planned on leaving her today. I have to work the rest of the week, so today I planned on enjoying her in the many rooms of my home, but if I flake out on my brothers now, I'll never hear the end of it.

"What about later?" She looks up and blinks those gorgeous blue eyes at me. I try to read her look. Hesitation? Interest? I shrug it off. I'm sure it's nothing more than mere curiosity at when I'm going to take her virginity. That'd be the only obvious thing on her mind. It's her entire purpose for being here.

I bend down to whisper near her ear, careful that my brothers don't overhear. "I quite enjoyed my cock in your mouth last night."

She swallows and lets out a tiny gasp, inaudible to anyone but me. The sound makes my dick flex in my pants. *Fuck*.

I raise one hand and stroke her cheek with the back of my knuckles. "You're really good at sucking cock, you know that, right?"

I check her eyes for her reaction, but this information looks like news to her. Okay, so maybe she's just good at sucking mine. Even better news. Her cheeks are rosy and pink and her eyes dart around me, checking to see if my brothers are listening to us. They are, but I'm sure they're acting like they're not.

She licks her lips, completely unaware how erotic that sight is to me. Is it possible to golf with a raging erection? Apparently I'm about to find out.

"Enjoy your day with Marta, but then be ready for me tonight." It's not a request and a she simply nods.

I head out with my brothers, tossing my clubs

into the back of Collins' SUV and then climb into the passenger seat. I'd completely forgotten about golf today. I hated golf, but Collins had joined the Beverly Hills country club to woo some stuffy client, and he'd been on me and Pace to join him for golf so he could feel like he was getting his money's worth at the overpriced club.

"So, are you fucking her, or what?" Collins asks before we're even out of my driveway, not wasting a second.

"Are we really going to talk about this like we're back in high school?" I ask, keeping my expression bored and fixed on the road.

"Fuck yeah we are." Pace leans forward between the seats, resting on the console. "She's hot and you know it. Hot enough that Collins forgot all about his supermodel girlfriend."

That was fucking funny. Nothing rattled Collins.

"No one would blame you if you were," Collins continues. "After what that redheaded bitch did to you."

Why in the fuck was everyone bringing up Stella? I bite down, tasting blood.

"I'm not fucking her," I answer. *At least not yet.* "She's my friend's sister," I remind them.

"Right, John from Harvard." Collins smirks. He knows just as well as I do that Sophie's not from the east coast. Why in the fuck had she said she was from Boston?

"Well, she's not my friend's sister, and I have a guest room in my condo. I'll take her if you don't want her," Pace replies, completely oblivious.

He's not taking her anywhere, but I'm not about to engage in a childish argument over my own property.

CHAPTER SIX

Sophie

With a name like Marta, I was expecting a dowdy older housekeeper type with a gray bun and sensible shoes, certainly not the twenty-something blonde who shows up in a cute sundress and strappy sandals with a Chanel bag slung over her shoulder.

"Sophie?" she asks, pulling off the large sunglasses that cover her eyes.

"Yes. Marta, I assume?"

She nods and extends her hand. "You do need a wardrobe, don't you?" Her gaze travels down my body, taking in Drake's baggy clothes and she bites her lip. Then she pulls a pair of cut off jean shorts and a tank top from her bag and hands them to me. "Colton said you'd need something to borrow for today."

"Colton?" I ask, accepting the clothes.

Her eyebrows pinch together. "Colton Drake? The man whose home you're staying in."

I nod. Colton Drake. Even his name is sexy. He hadn't exactly given me a fake name after all. I smile when I remember Pace calling him *Coco* this morning.

"Most of his staff calls him Mr. Drake." She shrugs. "But he's just Colton to me."

Interesting. I wonder what else she is to him. She's tiny and gorgeous with her tanned skin and blond curls and I feel self-conscious in her presence.

When I return from the guest bath down the hall, I'm dressed in the shorts and tank top, feeling thankful for something to wear, even if they are a little on the tight side, and then I retrieve my shoes from upstairs.

"Ready?" she asks.

I nod and follow her outside into the bright sunshine.

I climb into the little red sports car convertible

beside her, tugging at the too short shorts.

She presses a button near the rearview mirror and the roof lowers and folds back neatly into the trunk. I guess I'll need to get used to my new LA life.

"How did you say you knew Colton? He was kind of vague on the details," she asks, pulling out of his private drive.

I repeat the story that he and I settled on and she nods along without questioning me.

"What did Drake, I mean, Colton tell you about me?" I ask.

"He said that you'd be staying awhile and that you'd need pretty much everything."

"Oh." I get quiet as I look out at the scenic drive we're cruising down, remembering the phone call with my mom.

"Listen, Sophie, I know it's not my place to pry, but if you're in some kind of trouble, if you need anything…even a friend to listen…I'm happy to help."

I suppose it did sound suspicious. I'd showed up out of the blue without a stitch of clothing to spare. "No, it's nothing like that. Just a fresh start."

I smile, trying to lighten the mood.

"Well, the offer stands. And I know Colton better than anyone. It's not like him to just move a woman in."

I swallow and wonder what she means. I realize Marta could give me information about him, probably more than anyone else. I chew on my thumb nail until my curiosity gets the better of me. "How long have you worked for him?" I want to inquire about exactly what her role is, but I'm not sure if there's a polite way to word it.

"Oh gosh, Colton and I have quite the history. Where do I start?" She laughs and I glance over at her. Her smile is gorgeous, and her loose blonde waves drift around her face in the subtle breeze, but all I'm able to concentrate on is her implied familiarity with my new owner.

Have they slept together? Are they *currently* sleeping together? I don't know why it hasn't occurred to me before, but Colton has no obligation to be faithful to me. A thought that makes my stomach cramp. While I'm blowing him in private and giving him the most precious part of me, he could be off wining and dining other women. Beautiful, confident women like Marta with her easy smile and carefree attitude.

I knew this situation wasn't going to be ideal, but I also never imagined I'd be living with such an eligible young bachelor like Colton Drake. Already he's affecting me in ways I didn't anticipate.

"Mm, let's see. I've been his personal assistant for…" She purses her lips. "Six years now. I began at his office as a receptionist, but our personalities just clicked and I started working for him *personally* a short time after that. Having someone he can trust in his home and private life is important to him."

I nod, but the truth is, I don't know him at all. It's weird to think that I know what he looks like naked, but I don't actually *know him* know him. And I want to. Why is he so successful at such a young age and why in the world did he go to that auction in the first place? Questions burn through my mind like a raging inferno.

We spend the afternoon in various boutique shops, where I try on and purchase jeans, shorts, sundresses and tops, all on Colton Drake's gold card that Marta whips out at every transaction. For once I actually have money, but after Marta reprimanded me for trying to pay and said that Colton had instructed her everything was to go on his card, I stopped fighting it.

We already have several full shopping bags of clothes and are at our last stop of the day — a lingerie boutique for some much needed bras and panties.

I'm digging through a bin of simple cotton panties, the kind that fill my drawers back home when I sense Marta's presence beside me. She eyes the pretty pair of pale yellow boy shorts trimmed in lace and purses her lips. "Colton favors dark colors," she says.

My stomach twists again at her implied familiarity with the man I'm currently sharing a bed with. I want to argue, to tell her it's not like that between me and him, but instead, I drop the forgotten undergarment into the bin and continue looking. From the corner of my eye, I can see her eyeing me suspiciously. Maybe that was a test, and I've just answered her question about my relationship with him without saying a single word. Oh well. I do have a sexual relationship with him — or at least I am going to soon — and there'll be no sense hiding it.

Stocking up on basic black and navy bikini panties and matching bras, I find Marta browsing in the clearance area of the store. She doesn't seem the type to need to shop in the discount section, but

I secretly like that she's thrifty. I am too.

It's not lost on me that she's likely my best source of information on Colton. I mean, geez, I didn't even know his first name before she'd told me. I wondered what else I could get her to let slip.

When she sees me approach, she smiles at me again. "Ready?"

"I think so." I hold up an armful of undergarments. "But take your time." Today's been all about me so far, which is something I'm not used to. She can browse if she wants. "That's cute." I nod to the red demi bra she's holding.

"They don't have my size." She shoves it back onto the rack and keeps looking.

I gather my courage. "Marta?"

"Hm?" she says, holding up a sequined tank top.

"Who's Stella?"

Her eyes zip over to mine. "He told you about Stella?"

Shit. Her accusatory tone and icy stare are too much, that, or my conscious is too big. My gaze drops down to the floor. "Not exactly. His brothers stopped by this morning, and her name might have come up." And his bedroom smells like stale perfume and one half of his closet seems like it's been hastily emptied out, I mentally add. Not to mention there's something about him that I can't put my finger on. Has he been hurt before? Had his heart broken?

Marta continues perusing the rack of discounted bras, her brows pinched together like she's recalling a bad memory. "He's not been himself since Stella. She did a fucking number on him," she mutters under her breath.

I can't really imagine someone hurting the ever in control Colton Drake, but then again, I have no idea of his past, just like he has no idea of mine. But I intend to find out.

Several hours later, Marta drops me off at Colton's place. We bought so much, all of my shopping bags barely fit in her tiny backseat and trunk. Marta helps me carry them inside and up the stairs. She marches with purpose toward Colton's bedroom, like it's a familiar route. The little sting of curiosity is back. I also note that there's no question about where I'm staying—she didn't even pretend to assume it was in one of the guest rooms.

She sets the bags down inside the mammoth

closet and turns to face me. I offer to change out of the clothes she's let me borrow for the day, but she waves me off.

"Thanks for everything today."

She nods. "Of course. As a friend of Colton's, I'm sure we'll be seeing a lot of each other. And seriously, I meant what I said before—if you need anything—a friend to grab coffee with, or drinks, or just a female to talk to when he drives you insane…Call me." She grins.

I accept her cell phone number, wondering what she means about him driving me insane.

Once Marta leaves me alone, I feel a little awkward placing my clothes on the empty side of the closet that was once occupied by Stella's stuff. But maybe that's what Colton intends bringing me here—for me to replace whatever bad memories she left behind.

If that's what he wants, I'll do it. Heaven knows I'm running from my own baggage too. I'm here for the money, but as the knot that had permanently taken up residence in my stomach lessens with each passing hour, I realize that's not the only thing this new way of life can provide me.

Being here in LA, in this mansion, brings a

sense of relief from the constant worry and heart-ache I live with every day. I miss my family, well, mostly Becca and of course I worry about her health, but it's not relentlessly churning in my head like before.

I should feel guilty at this realization, but honestly, it's a relief.

CHAPTER SEVEN

Colton

Before we leave the country club, I stop in at the boutique gift shop. The frilly blue lace camisole and panty set hanging in the window catches my attention, making me recall Sophie's pale blue panties from last night. And like a ship to a beacon of light, I find myself heading straight toward them.

"Can I help you find something?" The sales girl asks from behind the counter, letting her gaze wander down my toned chest and halt at the area directly below my belt. "Something for your girl-friend, maybe?" she asks.

Her subtlety is lacking. All she sees when she looks at me is a fat cock and a fatter wallet. If I'm at this club, it means I have money, but after the red headed monster from hell, it repulses me to think about ever being with a woman like that again. Just because she throws a pretty smile my way and would drop to her knees at my command doesn't mean she can have my heart.

Girls like her are only interested in the lifestyle I can provide them—the wealth, the status—not the man inside. Which is why I'm not interested in anything more than what I've arranged with Sophie. Clean and separate from the rest of me. Sex and intimacy have no place together.

"I'm good, thank you." I know Marta will have everything covered today, but that doesn't stop me from looking around while I wait for Pace and Collins to finish in the locker room. I'm hot and tired after playing thirty-six holes of golf, but I'd much prefer shower at home where I can put on fresh clothes after, rather than here with a bunch of men. And I wasn't joking when I told Sophie to be ready for me when I got home. Last night's prelude wasn't enough. I haven't stopped thinking about her luscious mouth or perky tits once.

Moving past the rows of silk panties and lacey camisoles I stop beside a display of lotions and oils. Grabbing one of the bottles, I head to the register to pay.

"Nice choice," the cashier beams up at me.

Ignoring her, I check my Rolex. I wonder if Sophie and Marta are back yet. The sales girl, obviously annoyed at my lack of attention, despite her skin tight top unbuttoned to show off the top of her bra, stuffs my purchase into a gift bag and shoves it at me.

I find Pace and Collins in the grand foyer of the club, rehydrating with bottles of water. "You ready, ladies?" I ask.

Collins tosses me a bottle of water. "Come on," he says to Pace, "we've got to get princess home in time for his blowjob."

Yes, please.

The house is silent when I return and I wander the rooms downstairs, checking the den and kitchen before heading upstairs. Disappointment courses through me at the idea that she's not back yet. At least I can get a shower in before she returns. The least I can do is wash myself before I expect her to devour my cock.

Stripping my shirt off over my head as I head

toward my bedroom, I'm surprised to find Sophie sitting in the center of my bed with her phone in her lap and a frown on her face.

"Everything okay?"

She startles at my voice and drops her phone on the bed. Her gaze wanders lazily down my naked chest and her frowns falls away. *Good girl.*

"It's fine." She sets her phone beside her on the bedside table. I wonder if she was talking to someone from home again. "How was golf?"

"Hot. I'm going to shower."

She nods, her eyes not daring to stray from mine, though I can tell she's drawn to my body.

I wash quickly, without waiting for the water to warm, soaping up my chest, abs, under my arms and of course the parts of me I want her mouth on. Wrapping a towel around my hips, I enter the bedroom once again, but this time Sophie's gone. *The fuck?* Apparently we needed to cover some ground rules. Like rule number one, be naked and waiting on my bed for me at all times.

Releasing a frustrated sigh, I drop the towel and dress before heading downstairs to find her.

Sophie's sitting in the den, the same spot we sat

last night. Her legs are curled under her and she's holding a book in her lap. All I can think of when I enter this room is her on her knees in front of me, taking my dick deep into her warm mouth. Christ, it's been way too long since I've been laid.

Her eyes lift from the book and settle on mine when I sit down across from her.

"Find something good?" I nod toward the book in her hands, which I assume has come from my personal library.

"Emily Bronte." She holds up the cover of *Wuthering Heights* for me to see. It's a dark and twisted love story. Story of my damn life.

"Have you read it before?"

"In high school. But I don't remember much of it." Setting the book down on the cushion beside her, she folds her hands in her lap and looks at me expectantly. She's curious about what's going to happen next.

"Are you hungry?" I surprise her by asking.

She nods carefully. I'm starving after the long afternoon spent on the course and when I reach for her hand, she carefully places her palm against mine. I tell myself that it's important I get her comfortable with me, but in actuality, I just like touching her.

I lead her into the kitchen. Sunday is the only day I don't have a staff here to prepare meals, but Beth usually leaves me with enough leftovers to survive for one day without her. I find the fixings for club sandwiches left in plastic containers and labeled in Beth's efficient script. Turkey, strips of crisp bacon, avocado spread, gruyere cheese, and thick slices of tomato marinated in vinaigrette.

We assemble the sandwiches at the island and take our plates back into the den.

"I'm curious about why you're here…" I pause, watching her reaction. It's obviously for the money, but I can't figure out why a girl like Sophie would be desperate enough to sell herself. She's a clean cut, normal girl by all outward appearances. I strongly doubt she has gambling debts or a drug addiction to fund. I take a bite of my sandwich and wait for her to answer. Honestly, I have mixed feelings about finding out more about her and making this personal, but I'm too damn curious not to ask.

She seems hesitant at first and chews her food slowly, stalling for time. "My sister's sick," she says softly, so soft I can barely hear her. "Her care is very expensive," she continues. It isn't what I'm expecting and her honesty surprises me.

"The money…it will help?" I ask.

"Very much so," she whispers. I can tell she has mixed feelings about all this. As relieved as she seems at taking care of her sister, I sense there's some lingering guilt about leaving home during a time of hardship.

I have no intention of baring my soul as completely as she's done. I can't. I doubt she'd stick around if she knew the real reason she was here. And I'm certainly not ready to let her go, especially before I've fulfilled the promise of her sweet, tempting body.

Her answer makes me feel the tiniest bit less selfish. I may have spent a million dollars to bring her here for my own egocentric needs, but knowing the money is going toward a worthy cause helps my conscious the slightest bit. "So you sold the only thing of value you had to save her." It's more a statement than a question, but Sophie nods.

She's an interesting girl, and not at all how I assumed she'd be, watching her stand up on that auction block, defying us all by covering herself. She's sweet and timid and something in me knows I should be careful with her. I recall the way she slept against me last night, letting me spoon my body around hers and gripping my thumb like a newborn clings to its mother once sleep finally found her. Her selfless choice to come live here with me, a virtual stranger, strikes something within me. She is fearless. A woman worth knowing.

We eat in heavy silence, each of us seeming to process this new revelation about the nature of our relationship.

"How did you lose your virginity?" she asks.

I choke down the last bite of my sandwich and take a swig of water. *Shit*. Is she seriously asking me that? Though I suppose I'd rather answer questions about my past than explain why I'd bought her. "I was seventeen. On vacation in Italy with my family before I started my senior year of high school. I met a local girl and…" I lift one brow and Sophie chuckles.

What more was there to say? It still brought a smile to my mouth to think of Luciana. She was four years older and not afraid of her raw sexuality. The sex had been phenomenal. Though to be fair, *any* sex would have been phenomenal to the seventeen-year old me. Someone other than me touching my dick? Yes, please.

"How were things with Marta today? I trust you got everything you needed?"

She nods. "Yes, thank you. Marta's...*nice.*"

The way the word hesitantly rolls off her tongue tells me there's more she wants to say.

"She is," I confirm. She can also be tough as balls when she needs to be, which is why I trust her with my personal affairs. "She's a regular around here. She's in charge of my household staff and does any personal work I need her to as well."

Her eyes lift to mine. "Are you sleeping with her?"

"I don't think that's any of your business, Sophie." My voice holds the edge of a warning. Just because I'm being amiable and pleasant doesn't mean I'm going to discuss my personal life with her and she might as well get used to that. She's here for one purpose and maybe it's time we both remembered that.

Her gaze falls from mine and she shifts uncomfortably in her seat.

"Do you remember what I said to you just before I left today?"

She nods. "About my...my mouth."

I lift a hand to her cheek and brush away a stray crumb of bread, letting my thumb rub against her lower lip. Her mouth parts at my touch and she sucks in a breath. I hold her eyes with mine, running my thumb along her plump bottom lip. Her mouth is incredibly sexy. "The only thing I want you worried about when it comes to my cock is how deep you can take it." The double entendre causes her chest to flush with heat.

As a virgin, we both know my size will be difficult for her to accommodate at first. An idea that once bothered me, but now excites the fucking hell out of me. The challenge of her, the idea of being the first to conquer her, brings out the caveman-like instincts inside me. Big fucking time.

"Go upstairs and get ready for me." I rise from the sofa and offer her my hand. She takes it and rises to her feet. Goddamn, the tiny jean shorts she's in make her legs look too damn long. It's impossible not to picture what they'd look like wrapped around my back as I pound into her. I watch her walk away, her round ass swaying softly as she retreats. Holy hell.

After taking our plates to the kitchen, I join her upstairs.

Sophie's standing in the center of the room,

looking completely lost like she's waiting for my instruction. Just the way she looks at me makes me half hard. *Christ*.

I enter the room and stop several feet in front of her. "Take off your top."

She lifts the tank top from over her head and drops it on the floor beside her feet. Without waiting to be told, her fingers reach around to find the clasp to her bra and it too falls away. *That's a good girl*.

Her tits are gorgeous. Full C-cups and perky. I know they'd feel warm and weighty in my palms and my fingers itch to touch her soft curves. I'm all too aware that I haven't touched her yet, but knowing that she'll probably pull away or stiffen under my touch makes me hesitate. When I do finally touch her, I want her to arch into me and moan out my name. I want to pinch her nipples and watch her eyes darken with lust for me.

I strip off my own shirt and then pop open the button on my jeans to make more room for my growing cock. "Come here." I reach for her hand and she steps forward, sliding her palm against mine. Pulling her tightly against my chest, I circle one hand around the back of her neck, lifting her face to mine.

I press my mouth to hers and her lips softly part, accepting me. I run my tongue along the seam of her mouth until she opens against me, then I sweep my tongue inside, claiming her with a deep kiss. Her body goes lax in my arms and I love the lush feel of her breasts flattening against my chest. The skin to skin contact is exquisite.

My tongue rubs along hers and Sophie meets my kiss thrust for thrust. The intensity of the kiss sends a jab of lust straight to my groin. I'm unable to stop my hips from rocking into hers, my dick seeking friction against her warm belly. Not breaking our connection, I reach down and adjust myself, then find Sophie's hand and bring it to the bulge in my jeans. Without any further coaxing, her hand begins rubbing my length encased in denim, coaxing a low rumble from my throat when she squeezes me.

"Show me what that mouth can do again," I growl, breaking the kiss.

She drops to her knees on the carpeting and blinks up at me. Fuck, she's beautiful. The urge to reach down and fondle her tits, to feel her nipples harden under my touch is almost unbearable. But instead I undo my pants and I push the jeans and boxers down my legs, taking my cock in my right hand and offer it to Sophie.

Her mouth opens and her eyes remain on mine. I have no idea why that's such a turn on, but fuck, it is. I place the head of my cock between her lips and Sophie makes a soft sucking sound, the warmth of her tongue lapping at me briefly before I pull myself away again. "Show me your tongue."

She does, her flat, pink tongue waiting for me so enticingly. I rub the head of my dick against it, letting her saliva coat me and the sensitivity shoots straight to my balls. Pleasure rips through my veins and I stifle a groan. "That's it. Open wider."

Her jaw widens and I push myself into the hot cavern of her mouth, taking every bit of pleasure she can give me. Pumping my hips forward, I bump the back of her throat, dragging myself in and out of her mouth.

Sophie is a fucking champ at sucking dick. I hadn't been exaggerating before. Her gag reflex is practically non-existent, a skill I haven't encountered with many women, especially given my size. Her hands join the fun, wrapping firmly around my base and stroking as her mouth continues taking me deep. Good god this girl will be my undoing. I clench my ass muscles, fighting off the impending orgasm preparing to rip from my body. I'm going to come in her mouth again, and there's not a damn thing I can do to stop it.

I growl out her name and tangle my hands in her hair, pushing myself deeper down her throat as I explode. Sophie's eyes find mine and she watches me intently as I empty myself into her mouth. It's the most erotic sight and even as I pull myself free, my erection refuses to fade.

Christ, that was intense. If oral sex is off the charts with her, I can't imagine what penetration will be like. And that simple thought pumps a fresh round of blood south and I'm fully hard and ready again in a split second.

Taking her hand in mine, I lift her to her feet. Her mouth is swollen and pink, her lips full. I kiss her lightly. "Stay right here."

I cross the room and retrieve the gift bag from the top of my bureau. I remove the small bottle of oil from the bag and Sophie's eyes zero in on it, and then dart down to my still eager erection and she swallows roughly. Her entire body stiffens. She looks terrified. *What the hell?*

"Everything okay?" I don't understand her reaction.

I look down at the bottle of oil I bought earlier

and realize she must think its lubricant. As if I'd just roughly lube up my dick and push into her before she was ready. My gut drops to the floor. I feel like a grade-A asshole. The last thing I want her to feel is fear. "It's massage oil." I lift the bottle to show her. "We're not fucking tonight, sweetness."

Her relief is instant. She draws a deep shuddering breath and her shoulders sag.

How in the fuck had I ever thought I could go through with this? The idea of forcing her into having sex with me is deplorable. Christ what was wrong with me? But this was exactly why I hadn't wanted a virgin. I'd wanted a girl who was down to fuck — not some terrified young thing I'd have to treat with kid gloves.

Drawing a deep breath of oxygen into my lungs, I push away any and all erotic thoughts of taking her and pull on my boxer briefs. I won't touch her until I know it's what she wants. But I don't think I can go without her hot mouth around my dick. Now that I know she's okay sucking cock and how well she excels at it—there's no way I'm giving that up. I'm not that fucking generous. I have needs and I've paid royally to have them serviced.

"Lay down on your stomach." I point to the chaise lounge chair. She may not be ready for me to touch her sexually, but I plan to return the physical pleasure she's given me in another way.

She lays down right in the center, and I lift her body to the side, making room so I can sit beside her. She turns her head to the side so she can glance up at me, curious about what I'm going to do.

Pouring some of the oil into my hand, I rub my hands together to warm it before applying it to Sophie's back. Her skin is soft, but her muscles are tense. Which is exactly why I need to start off my physical contact with her slowly and let her get accustomed to me touching her body.

She feels small and delicate under my hands. I rub the oil into her skin, sinking my fingers into her flesh and rubbing out the knots in between her shoulder blades. Sophie releases a soft grunt when I apply more pressure. "Is this okay?" My voice comes out huskier than I intend.

"Yeah," she breathes.

I run my fingers down the slope of her spine, admiring the twin dimples in her lower back just above her firm round ass.

"Colton…" she breathes, her mouth curling up in a happy little smile.

Marta must have told her my name. I like the sound of it on her lips.

After rubbing out all the knots, I lightly massage her neck, digging my fingers into her scalp. She was tense when I first began, but now her body is limp and relaxed for me. "Does this feel good?"

"Mmmm," she moans. The sound goes straight to my ever present erection, and the beast flexes in my boxers, as if to remind me it's still there. It seems he's going to be a permanent fixture when Sophie's around.

Looking down at her creamy bare skin and knowing she's topless makes it hard to concentrate, but I do my best at rubbing her back, working my way down her spine until I'm massaging her lower back. The breathy noises she makes are distracting as fuck and the tiny shorts she's wearing taunt me. I want to turn her over and push my fingers inside her, feel how tight and warm she is. Of course I can't. Yet. If I win her trust first, the sex will be that much better. At least that's what I tell myself.

CHAPTER EIGHT

Sophie

When I crawl into bed beside Colton that night, I feel boneless and relaxed. It never occurred to me that two days into my new living situation I'd still be a virgin, have an entire wardrobe full of new clothes and be at the receiving end of the best massage I've ever had in my life.

I slip under the sheets, thankful they're cool against my overheated skin. Pleasuring him like that—feeling his taut muscles under my fingertips, inhaling his musky scent, watching him come apart, I can't deny it's a turn-on. He's so in control, so masculine, it's a potent combination, one that my own libido stands up and takes notice of.

Colton reaches over and with one hand, drags

me closer, just like he did the night before, spooning his big, firm body around mine. I feel him release a sigh against my ear. "Night, sweetness," he murmurs, sounding half-asleep.

I know it's totally strange and I shouldn't let my guard down so quickly or easily, but I trust him. I just do. Maybe it's the way he looks at me, or maybe it's because he hasn't taken anything that isn't his to take, but regardless, a little sense of ease has wormed its way into my head, allowing me to relax in his presence. Maybe it's because I know things could have turned out so much worse. God, part of me still can't believe I'd gone through with that auction. I knew it was crazy, but exchanging six months of my life to give Becca a shot at the life she deserves made it a no-brainer. It'd be stupid not to do this. And honestly, I'd never been one of those girls who held onto her virginity out of principle. I just hadn't had a serious boyfriend with all the turmoil of my family life and I wasn't going to just give it to anyone. I guess it turned out for the best — now that man would be Colton, which wasn't necessarily a bad thing, he was freaking gorgeous, and I was helping my sister in the process.

I'm just about to fall asleep, feeling at peace with my decision, when a sudden thought jars me from my peaceful reverie. What if all this...the kindness, the no-sex thing, maybe he's trying to lull me into a false sense of security, to get me to trust him so I submit to him completely. The mystery of his past is still bugging me too. There's Marta and Stella, both of whom I want to understand his relationship with.

And it's not like he's a saint—I've pleasured him twice at his command, dropping to my knees to suck him off. God, he's no prince charming. *Get a grip, Sophie.* I will need to stay on my guard a bit more after all.

Realizing all of this while laying snuggly in his arms, I distance myself the tiniest bit, fluffing the pillow under my head to get more comfortable. I take a deep breath, feeling calmer and more in control almost immediately. I won't let myself get so sucked into his world I can't see straight. I may have sold my body as a sex slave, but my heart, my mind, my spirit are all still mine. I still want to be Sophie when this is all said and done. If I'm to survive my six months with him, I need to remember I'm playing a role—living out a very expensive fantasy he's created—nothing more. Ignoring the ache pleasuring him created between my thighs, I close my eyes and try to relax.

My body's natural physical reaction and my growing attraction to him causes my blood to pound in my ears. It's not something I can control, which both excites and confuses me. Perhaps it's my limited experience, but my body's sexual response to his nearness is unexpected and frustrating, especially because he seems in no rush to do anything about it. Sharing his bed, being the one to pleasure him makes me want to discover my own body's pleasure. But for now, I clamp my thighs tightly together and pray for sleep to take me.

Colton

I shouldn't have forced Sophie to her knees last night. For all the pleasure I derived, it's been overshadowed by guilt, which ratchets up with each passing hour. I feel like a fucking schmuck.

When she cowered away from my touch last night, it put everything into perspective. I don't do regrets or self-loathing, so needless to say I'm distracted and edgy all day long. I bark orders to my assistant, I'm short with clients and skip several of my meetings. All due to my shitty mood. The strange thing is, I don't regret buying her. That fuckwad at the auction would have taken her home if I hadn't. And I don't even want to know the sick things that bastard had planned. I'd overheard him bragging before the auction began about his playroom, complete with whips, restraints and canes. A girl as soft and pure as Sophie wouldn't have lasted the night in his company. At least there's solace in knowing I haven't ruined her. Yet.

As I cruise up the hilly road toward my private drive, I glance out at the sun sinking into the Pacific Ocean. It's a view I'll never tire of, even if this house is tainted with memories of the biggest mistake of my adult life. *Stella.*

Just thinking of her puts a bad taste in my mouth and I force my thoughts to return to my situation with Sophie. Watching the last sliver of orange dip below the horizon, I vow to exercise more self-control. Just because I've bought her doesn't mean I need to violate her with every passing thought. *Christ.* I wince realizing that's exactly what I've been doing.

I know all too well what it's like to have your trust and sense of well-being completely fucking shattered and I won't be responsible for taking anything from Sophie she's not willing to give. If and when we fuck—it'll be because she wants it. My devious mind immediately launches into various scenarios where I can entice her to want it… *Fuck.* Abstaining is going to be harder than I thought. Excuse the pun.

CHAPTER NINE

Sophie

As my feet pound the pavement, my breath pushes past my parted lips and my underarms and lower back grow damp with perspiration. I've been here a week and it feels nice to be back in the familiar routine of jogging. I lose myself in the rhythm of my feet thumping dully against the pavement. Despite the heat, it feels good to use my body. My lungs scream at me, my muscles pushed to the limit and yet, I make a silent promise to myself. *One more mile.*

As I jog, my mind wanders to Colton as it so often does. My brain recalls and catalogs a million little facts about him. How warm he is curled around me at night, the heavy thud of his heartbeat against my back as he drifts off to sleep, the curious way he watches me move about his home like he enjoys seeing someone—*me*—in his space. There's something I like about it too. I feel free from the constant worry over Becca. Of course I still think of her constantly, wondering about her treatment and pray that she's going to be okay, but part of me likes not having to face it every day.

Despite his silence and relative disregard for me, there are lots of little things about my new master I'm growing fond of. The deep rasp of his sleep-laced voice in the morning, the way he always sets out a cup and saucer for my morning coffee before he leaves for work, the slow curl on his mouth when he treats me to a rare smile.

He's not an over-eager, fumbling man in anything he does. He's sure, calculated and strong. Which to me is incredibly sexy. Remembering the soft brush of his mouth against mine the few times he'd kissed me, and the confident way he'd handled his large cock, placing it on my tongue and silently groaning out his release… all the muscles below my belly button clench and I fight to maintain my balance.

Even though I know I shouldn't let my mind go there, I know he wouldn't be anything like the teenage boys I dated in the past—with pizza breath and fumbling hands. He'd be confident and sure when he touched me. He is magnetic, charismatic and charming. It's an irresistible combination and one that I'd be defenseless against—*if* it ever happened.

Even if I don't understand this man, or his reasons for bringing me here, I appreciate his unexpected tenderness toward me. My living situation could be a lot worse and I'm grateful for him and for the money that means my sister has a fighting chance at life.

A slow smile uncurls on my lips as I realize I've passed the mile marker. With thoughts of Colton to distract me, running is a breeze.

As I circle back toward the house, I see Marta's little red sportscar pulling away and she gives me a wave before zooming off down the driveway. I hadn't known she was stopping over today. She usually comes in the mornings, checks on the work of the house staff and then leaves to do whatever it is she does for Colton.

When I reach the house, I stumble inside, grateful to feel the cool air conditioning against my overheated skin. I slump to the floor in the mudroom, sucking in deep breaths, and tug off both shoes. Colton's suit coat is laying on the bench.

He's home? Maybe that explains Marta's late afternoon visit. I know I should straighten my disheveled appearance—fix my ponytail that is half out already, but as I sit there trying to calm my ragged breathing, I get the sense of being watched.

"Hey there, sweetness," Colton's rich voice rasps over my flushed skin and my eyes jerk up to his. He's leaning casually against the door frame, one ankle crossed over the other. His shirt is unbuttoned at the collar and he looks both happy and relaxed. My eyes are unfortunately drawn to the front of his dress pants, which refuse to lay flat over the impressive bulge he sports. Heat flares up my spine as I wonder what he and Marta were up to. He's never been home this early before, and I can't help but think her being here isn't just some random coincidence. "Have a nice run?" he asks, his dimple peeking at me from one cheek.

"Uh huh." I nod, still utterly out of breath.

He enters the room, stepping closer and frowns down at the running shoes I've kicked off. I had my mom send me a package with a few things I missed from home. Mainly these shoes and my iPod for running. He toes one of the shoes, flipping it over, with a frown on his full lips. "These are what you wear to run?"

He checks for my reaction and I nod again. "They're comfy." I know they're old but they do the trick. They're worn in all the right places.

"There's no tread left on them. No support. You need a new pair every few hundred miles. How long have you been running in these?"

I'm guessing "since high school" is the wrong answer. My parents bought me these when I joined the cross country team my senior year. "A while."

"I'll give you my credit card, you can order a new pair and have them delivered." His tone is direct and there's something I dislike about being told what to do. I'm here on my own accord, making my own choices. Running is one of them. "If I want a new pair of shoes, I'll get them. I don't need you buying me anything."

His brows squeeze together like this is a foreign concept to him. *Geez*. Just because he has money, doesn't mean I'm okay with using him or taking advantage of his hospitality. What kind of women did he date in the past?

"If I'm offering the help, why refuse it?" he asks.

"Because I like taking care of myself." I silently add that I don't need a man to provide all of my needs. Despite selling my body into this jacked up arrangement, I am a strong, smart, independent woman. I wouldn't compromise on that.

He raises his hands in front of him in a silent peace offering. "Okay. I'm sorry. I just don't want you to twist your ankle. These have no support left in them."

His concern softens me. He offers me a hand, and I accept, letting him propel me off the floor and to my feet. Now that we're standing face to face, I'm self-conscious about my sweaty skin — the droplets of perspiration that still clung to my upper lip and between my breasts. I want to ask him why he's home early, but he distracts me, lifting a damp lock of hair from my neck and tucking it carefully behind my ear. The brush of his fingertips against my neck sends a chill zipping down my spine. His touch lingers there, stroking the column of my throat and my collarbone as if to test my reaction. His finger runs from my neck down to the tops of my breasts which heave with each ragged breath I draw into my overworked lungs.

"You need to understand you're mine to look after," he says, his voice rough and full of need.

That had never been explicitly part of our arrangement and we both know it. But somehow, along the way, his concern for me has grown. I'm not about to complain, I just stand here, transfixed by these new and developing feelings growing between us.

The rush of his fingertips against my hot skin force my eyelids to drift closed. Most of my life, everyone's focus and attention had been on Becca—as it should be, but here, in his presence, I'm the one that matters. His attention feels nice.

But just as quickly as he began touching me, his hand drops away and he takes a step back.

"I'm going to shower," I exhale.

He nods, still looking down at me like there's more he wants to say.

I exit the mudroom and head for the stairs.

Colton

Seeing Sophie after her run, breathing hard from exertion and pink as a berry makes me want things I told myself I couldn't have. She's not really mine, so none of this should matter to me, yet it does, tremendously.

I head to my office, needing to relieve some sexual tension. It would be so easy to fall into familiar routines. I could make one phone call, fuck, I could even just send a one-line text and have Marta back over here, ready and willing to suck me off. Lord knows she'd do it. Probably drop everything and jump at the chance.

Though it'd been a long ass time since we'd done anything like that, the way she still occasionally looks at me, her eyes wandering over my toned chest and abs told me she'd be up for some genital-on-genital contact. Even after I'd told her that despite what had happened in the past, she and I needed to remain on a professional level, she'd kept herself single all these years, waiting, silently watching my relationship with Stella build, and then fall apart. But I knew if I made that call, I wouldn't get the satisfaction I was seeking, and I'd end up feeling worse. Regret would churn somewhere deep inside me. I don't want Marta. I want Sophie. And ever since my life—or at least my love life—went down the tubes two years ago, I vowed to live life with no regrets, so it was back to the original plan.

This line of thinking reminds me of the conversation I had with Sophie the other night. Her sister's illness, just like my previous harrowing experience puts your life into perspective. It makes you weigh the things in your life, and put everything under a microscope—what you're doing, how you spend your days. After I found out the truth about Stella, I could have easily spiraled into a heavy-drinking male whore. Instead I threw myself further into my work and my charity. Doing anything else would have put me on the same level as her. And I wanted to be better than that, shit, I *needed* it.

My brothers' conversation comes flashing back to the forefront. They were shocked to hear I wasn't sleeping with Sophie, but they don't know the half of it. They'd be stunned to learn I haven't had a single partner in two years—that I've been living a celibate life, devoting myself only to my work. They'd be even more shocked to learn that Stella wasn't the one still holding things up between us. I was. And I had my reasons. Reasons I hoped to figure out and finally deal with soon. Maybe then I can finally put the past behind me and build a future—a concept that both excites and scares the fuck out of me.

I sink down into my office chair and click on my computer.

The first order of business is to get some sexual relief.

Sophie

After I emerge from my shower, scrubbed clean and hair neatly combed, I dress and head downstairs to find Colton. Every little insignificant moment we share—like earlier in the mudroom when I refused his offer for new shoes and he looked at me with reverence in his eyes, like I was some strange creature he'd never before encountered, I can feel us growing closer. Our connection, however odd and undefined, is growing deeper with each passing day I spend here. It's the last thing I expected. And my attraction to him is off the charts, making my body's reactions more intense and harder to ignore.

When I near his office, I hear voices from within. *Is someone in there with him?* The door's been left partially open, so I knock once and push it the rest of the way open, registering the sounds just as I enter the room. Dual feminine moaning coming from his computer. He clicks a button on his keyboard, silencing the noise in an instant. *Oh my god. Is he watching porn?* He's seated at his desk in the huge leather chair, but his face gives nothing away. His eyes smoldering on mine are the only thing I can see.

My face heats with the secret knowledge that while I'd been upstairs in his shower, he'd snuck down here to watch some girl on girl action. Was he pleasuring himself here in the confines of his office? *Don't look down.* I refuse to let my eyes fall to his lap. My curiosity is going to get me in trouble someday. What he does in here is his business. But if he has needs and desires, why not just come to me like he did in the beginning? Surely even a bad blowjob is better than his own hand, right? Apparently not. The rejection stings more than it has any right too. But the strange notion that he's cheating on me worms its way into my head, however irrational.

"Did you need something?" he asks, his voice deep and slightly breathless.

"I…" Why had I come down here? When I didn't find him in the kitchen, or the den, my feet led me to his office. There was no denying I looked forward to his company in the evenings. I pause and start again. "I was just wondering why you're home early."

He lets out a heavy sigh pushes his hands into his hair. "I had something I wanted to take care of."

As soon as he's says it, my mind dives into the gutter. Had he come home early to do this?

"Are you hungry?" he asks, his posture straightening.

"Sure."

He rises from the desk and leads me to the dining room. Apparently we aren't going to discuss his failed masturbation attempt, or that I'd overheard him watching porn.

"Have a seat," he says, motioning to the dining table. "I'll be right back."

Normally we carry the dinner dishes that Beth leaves for us together into the dining room, but him serving me feels nice. I pull out my usual chair, the one next to his spot at the head of the table, and plop myself down. I feel so confused and hot all over. What is happening to me?

Colton soon returns with our plates and glasses of sparkling water, topped with sliced lemon. After my run, I feel like I can eat just about anything, but the food smells amazing.

We each dig in, the comfortable silence of routine settling over us.

At night is the time I have to ask him questions and get inside his head a bit. I'm pondering what to ask him about tonight when I notice him frowning at me.

"Why aren't you eating?" he asks.

I look down at the pasta primavera on my plate. He's right. I've barely touched it.

"Is everything okay with your sister?" he asks, setting his own fork down beside his plate.

I take a sip of water and lick my lips. "Yeah. Things are okay. She starts her first round of treatment this week."

He nods thoughtfully.

I can't help but think I've infiltrated his life, his routines, with my own baggage. Maybe I should never have told him about Becca, because the way he looks at me now is like a sad, exploited girl.

"Do you regret bringing me here?" I blurt.

"Why would I?" he asks, his brows drawing together.

Because you haven't laid a finger on me in days, because you bought me to take my virginity and I'm still as pure as they come? I shrug. "Nevermind, forget I said anything." An uncomfortable silence fills the room and we each continue picking at the food on our plates. "So, I've been wondering. Why don't you don't have a girlfriend?" I ask next.

He takes a sip of his drink, stalling for time.

Colton

Sophie is watching me expectantly, waiting to hear about my relationship status. It's not something I'm ready to discuss with her now, or possibly ever. Every damn muscle in my body is strung so tight I feel like I'm going to spontaneously combust. I'd been distracted as fuck at work again today, and came home to get a little relief in the form of an orgasm. Only I'd failed at that too.

I look up into the sweetest, most innocent pair of blue eyes I've ever seen and draw a shuddering breath. Sure, my last relationship had ended in disaster, but just because a beautiful, well-spoken, sweet woman is sharing my home, it shouldn't turn me into a pile of hormonal goo at a basic question.

I need to man up. She's seven years younger than me. I'd bought her for fuck's sake. It makes me feel a bit like a creepy old man. Even though something tells me that's not how she views me.

No, when she looks at me I can see the pulse thrum in her neck, her cheeks blushing like a ripe berry. There is some chemical reaction, a basic attraction between us. She feels it. I feel it. Yet we both ignore it.

In my darker fantasies, I'd eat a girl like her for breakfast, but as I've gotten to know her and forced myself to take things slow, a different side of me was emerging. He is kinder, more patient, and open to exploring the possibility of a woman in his life for the first time in a long time. I like him.

Sophie's still watching me across the table, still waiting to hear my response about why I'm single.

"I guess no one's caught my interest in a while," I answer. It's the truth. I hadn't been looking for anything serious. Regular sex was the only thing I was missing — hence my impulse buy at the auction. I'd been in San Francisco for business when I learned about the auction — and bored, or just lonely, I'd gone if only to see what the fuss was about. I never truly expected to walk away with a woman on my arm. But Sophie's trusting eyes had implored mine, silently begging me to get her out of there.

"Come on, what's the real reason you're single?" she presses on.

"Not discussing that."

"Play along. Just let me in a little, and in turn, I'll answer anything you want to know." She smiles adoringly, batting her eyelashes.

Her offer is enticing. I wouldn't mind getting deeper inside her head. If she wants the truth, I'll fill her in. "In my experience women are interested in two things. Money and power."

She opens her mouth to protest and I hold up a hand stopping her. "You wanted to know."

She motions for me to continue, then folds her hands in her lap.

"You can argue all you want, but I'm not just speaking about the women in my life. It's biology. Have you ever studied evolutionary science?" She shakes her head. "Women are looking for the biggest, baddest caveman out there—a provider to protect her and her offspring. It's simple science."

She seems to accept my line of thinking and I continue, after taking another swig of my drink.

"They want a well-hung, devoted husband whose wealth can afford them the type of lifestyle they dream of. He works all day, slaving away to make a living while his trophy bride is fucking the pool boy." *Or gardener, as it were.* A kid barely out of high school who wouldn't know what to do with his dick in his hand. "She has everything she ever dreamed of, but she gets bored spending her darling husband's money all day and soon needs a new toy — something fun and dangerous to distract herself with. If it's not the pool boy, then its pain pills and wine-spritzers at ten am. Trust me, Sophie, this is the world I grew up in. I know it well."

That last comment has her looking at me like she's wondering about my own upbringing. Actually, my mom was so in love with my dad she never strayed, as far as I knew, and she passed away much too early. My dad was unfortunately the philanderer who couldn't keep from humping his secretary. Just another reason why I don't believe in the sanctity of marriage. I've seen it fucked six ways from Sunday.

I'd done everything I could think of to make Stella happy. The finest clothes, expensive jewels, flashy cars, taking her on dream vacations, yet nothing made her truly happy. Even coming home from work early to surprise her — she'd complain that I was interrupting her afternoon ritual. It left me messed in the head. I couldn't do a thing right where women were concerned. Except in the bedroom. I never had any complaints there.

"Men think women are complex, and they are, but for the most part, they want to be left the fuck alone with his credit card." I drop my napkin to the table and push away my plate, my appetite vanishing.

Her posture straightens. "That's not true at all. Maybe for some women, some horrible, deceitful women, but for most, they want passion, to be desired, loved and cherished." Her voice drops, going all whisper soft, and I realize she's giving me a glimpse at what she herself desires from a mate.

I release a slow breath. There's no sense in arguing with her. "Can I ask you a question?" I say.

She nods.

"When you asked if I regretted bringing you here...do you regret going to the auction? Coming home with me?"

"No." Her voice is sure, steady. "I did what I had to do for my sister, and..." She drops her chin to her chest like she doesn't want to continue.

I lift her chin with two fingers and force her eyes back up to mine. "Tell me."

She swallows, the long column of her throat moving in a pretty way. "This is going to sound weird."

"Try me."

She draws a deep breath and releases it slowly. "I've never had the luxury of time and space like this before—something just for me."

I can see what she means. Sleeping in and jogging and swimming every day has been good for her. Her skin is kissed in a sunbathed glow and her body is equal parts relaxed and toned. It's a look that suits her.

Sophie fishes the lemon slice from her water glass and brings it to her lips, sucking the sour juice in the most distracting way. *Fuuuck.*

She sets the lemon slice down. *Thank God.* And continues. "I was always the twin sister of the girl who had cancer. I never had my own identity. And even though I'm not there yet, this time away has given me some much needed perspective. It's like there is life beyond hospital rooms and the crippling stress. It's making me see that I wasn't even truly living before. And I should be. If Becca's illness has taught me anything, it's that life can be taken away from you in an instant. I've been wasting mine. And even though I don't know what's next, I know I don't want to continue to live like

I was."

It's deeper than I intended her to go, but I like hearing all of her inner thoughts. "What else?" I ask.

"I want to have a career I'm passionate about, I want to fall in love, travel the world, make lasting friendships…You know, basically conquer the world and have the best life ever. I hope Becca is right alongside me, but even if I have to go it alone, I will. For her." She smiles sadly up at me.

"Sounds like a brilliant plan. Let me know how I can help."

After dinner, I head over to Collins' place for a mid-week drink with my brothers, needing the distraction. My cock feels like it's about to explode every time I'm in the same room as Sophie.

I find them sitting outside by the pool, a bottle of expensive bourbon sitting on the table between them. Seems like I'm not the only one having a long week.

I slide into the lounge chair and Pace hands me a glass, filling it generously with liquor. "Bottoms up, baby."

"What's the occasion?" I ask.

Collins shrugs. "Tatianna's talking about wanting an engagement ring. Leaving pictures of huge diamond rings all over the damn house."

"And?" I hadn't realized their relationship was all that serious, even though she's lived with him for about six months now. I figured it was more a relationship of convenience. When they started dating, she needed a place to stay, and he needed regular sex. Problem solved.

He looks down into his glass thoughtfully. "How are things going with the roomie?" Collins asks instead of answering.

"Fine."

"And how's her job search going?"

"Good."

Collins rolls his eyes. My one word responses aren't going to fly with him. He started it though by dodging my question about Tatianna.

"Have you fucked her yet?" Pace asks, much less tactfully.

I choke on a swig of bourbon and clear my

throat. "No." My voice is gruff. It's not that I haven't thought about it. I have. Almost constantly. I imagine lifting her up with her ass in my hands until her legs hug my waist. Pressing my fingers to her warm center while biting the soft skin at her throat. The waiting and wanting is pure torture. Christ, I'm screwed. How did I not think this through when I brought her home?

"No shit?" Both he and Collins turn to face me, like this is breaking news.

"Please tell me you're not still hung up on Stella," Collins asks, his sympathetic eyes locked on mine.

Fuck no. I'm not hung up on her. I'm just trying to do the right thing — without having one fucking clue what that means.

They watch me, cataloging my contemplative mood and Pace chews on his lower lip. "Seriously dude, Stella is ancient history, even if she refuses to get the fuck out of your life, there's nothing wrong with moving on."

"I know that," I grumble. I've told myself the same thing, over and over, yet some unknown force holds me back. Of course they don't know it's been two fucking years since I've been intimate with a woman, and being in such close proximity to a beautiful girl like Sophie is the worst kind of torture.

"So, what's the hold up, man? I'd be tapping that sweet pussy every night." Pace gives me a goofy grin.

"She's a virgin." As soon as I've said it, I want to take it back. It's too intimate a piece of knowledge to share with them. It's Sophie's personal business. I don't tell them how I've come to possess this information, or that I'd bought the right to that particular privilege; I just sit there staring down into my now empty glass, wondering if and when I'll do something about it.

"Wow." Collins says while Pace's cocky grin widens. *Asshole*. "Not what I was expecting you to say," Collins continues, "I thought you'd feed us that line again about her being your buddy's little sister." He grins wickedly.

Oh yeah. I'd almost forgotten the story I gave them. Just another testament to how messed up my head is right now.

"We all know things aren't totally finished with Stella, so I'm not going to pretend like they are, but really, is that honestly what's stopping you?" Pace asks, his eyes full of genuine confusion.

"I don't know." It's partly that—partly that I'm not sure if Sophie wants me, or if I even deserve to take something so precious from her. Part of it is her innocence, the sweet way her eyes follow me around the room, her trusting nature, the self-lessness she displayed to save her sister in the first place…she's entirely too good for me to use for my own pleasure. I already feel guilty—but after? I know I'll feel guilty as fuck. And even though I tell my brothers nearly everything, my participation at that auction is something I'll take to the grave. Not for my own sake, but because I doubt Sophie would want anyone knowing she'd sold herself that way.

"You need to figure it out, bro." Pace slaps me on the back before pouring another measure of liquor into my glass. "Otherwise I have a feeling you're in for a massive case of blue balls."

He's not kidding. I'm certain I have enough pent up semen to father three-quarters of the world's population. My dick aches constantly and my brain swirls with thoughts I shouldn't be having, but worst of all is the way my heart beats faster when she's near and all my senses tune into her completely.

My life for the past two years has been a lesson in order and self-control. I worked hard, and logged long hours at the gym, but I haven't been really living. Sophie's brought out a different side to me. Just the act of her curling around me at night had softened me, made me remember life wasn't only about coping. There were things worth living for. I wanted more of that mixed in.

CHAPTER TEN

Sophie

The mid-morning sunshine and the fact that there's still a warm male tucked against my side, remind me that it's Saturday. I stretch leisurely in the bed, already daydreaming of the delicious frothy cappuccino I'm going to make myself. I feel quite proud that I've mastered that damn over-pretentious coffee machine. It only took me three weeks.

Colton surprises me by reaching out and tugging me back against him. I'm greeted by a rather impressive erection nudging my backside. Gah! It's warm and solid and my body clenches uselessly, responding automatically at the mere thought of him.

Aside from those first two nights, we've had

no other sexual contact. I should feel relieved, but instead I find myself increasingly frustrated and confused. Almost a month has passed. I had figured he would take my virginity right away, but after several days and then weeks, I've become increasingly anxious and curious about it. Now I just want to get it over with, I'm tired of waiting and wondering when he's going to do. I was purchased as a sex slave and I know I'm not living up to my end of the bargain.

In the evenings he stays up late, working in his office and all but ignores me. Does he not find me attractive? Is he gay? Were my blowjobs that bad? The wait is maddening. Is there something wrong with me that my master refuses to fuck me? The belly churning anticipation is worse than the actual event. I need to get this over with. I'd often suspected he took care of his needs during his morning shower, but I've never been brave enough to venture into the bathroom for confirmation.

At first I wondered if he was waiting for me to make a move, to climb into his lap, or kiss him… but I know that's not it. He wasn't shy about taking what he wanted from me the first two times. He'd ordered me to my knees, undone his pants and stroked himself while I'd watched. I knew he wasn't timid, which made this all the more confusing.

You could cut the sexual tension between us with a knife — it's a real and visceral need permeating the air around us. And each night I'm expected to cuddle up to a shirtless, buff, delicious smelling man, lay in his arms and be the perfect little obedient bedmate. The problem with all this? It's fucking confusing. He's spent a million dollars to bring me here, and I'm all too aware of the money — every time I call home, when I hear about Becca's progress, every time I wander the various rooms of his mansion, or catch my reflection in the mirror and remember where my new designer wardrobe came from, it sends another wave of confusion rattling through me. I need to know what's expected of me — where we stand — what this arrangement involves.

His cock is the only part of him I clearly understand. It's less discreet in its desires. But his mind is like a fucking maze. One I have no hope of ever solving. I've thought about confronting him. But in this moment — feeling his hot arousal press against me, I want something else entirely.

A low rumble escapes his throat as he presses closer, his cock nestling in against my ass cheeks. Warm need dampens my panties, making them cling to my sensitive folds. He pushes his hips closer again, stealing my breath as I feel every hard ridge of him. His hand moves along my belly, inching its way upward and I hold my breath, wondering where it will land.

Wishful thinking takes hold and I angle my body toward his, wanting to feel his firm hand cup my breasts, rub against my sensitive nipples. His fingers splay open and brush the underside of my breast.

His breathing remains even and steady against the back of my neck and he's making sleepy little noises, which only urge me on. As much as I wish I could see his face, I'm too afraid to move — too afraid it will break the spell. I consider pushing my t-shirt up out of the way to help him, craving the skin to skin contact against my breasts and nipples, but instead, I press my bottom back into his hard arousal and he releases a grunt. The sound makes all my inner muscles clench.

"Soph?" he asks, his voice sleepy and rough.

Oh god. He was still asleep, and now I'm mortified.

I roll toward him and look down between us to where his cock is straining against his boxers, trying to come out and greet me.

Just let me take care of it for goodness sake.

I place my hand over his heart and feel its steady thump.

"Sorry, it's just morning wood," he says, noticing my fascination with what's below his navel.

"It's okay," I whisper. "Do you…Are you…" *Spit it out, Soph.* My lack of experience means I have no idea how to ask for what I want. I consider dipping my hand below his waistband, taking his firm cock in my fist and stroking him. I want him to kiss me, and pin me to the bed with his big body. Instead, he continues watching me with a little crease etched between his brows. He looks at me like I'm an amusing child that he has no idea what to do with.

"I'll take care of it," he says, climbing from bed and leaving me wet and so turned on I could scream in frustration.

I'm bored as shit.

In the weeks since I moved in, I've developed

a routine—one that bores me to tears—but at least it's a routine. I wake mid-morning when Colton's been gone to work for hours, have breakfast and coffee at the kitchen island while I talk to Beth, Colton's personal chef, then I change and sit outside in the sun, curling up in one of the lounge chairs on the balcony while I read.

Later, I either go for a swim in the pool or jog on one of the treadmills in the gym. From there, my day unravels a bit. I wander the house, take a nap, text with Becca, and basically just wait around for Colton to get home. It's a bland existence. I want to get a job—I need something to occupy my days other than thoughts of Colton and my strange new life.

The silver lining to all this is that Becca has been entered into the trial program and is receiving aggressive doses of medication that make her feel weak and sick but seem to be working. It's much too early to tell if they'll send her late stage cancer into remission, but we're all hopeful. And while I don't regret my decision, I have five more months to go, and I don't think I can take another day of this complete mental and emotional boredom. I need more stimulation.

At six o'clock, all of the household staff is

gone, and I'm showered and dressed and waiting for Colton to arrive home from work. Grabbing the little LED display remote, I tap the keypad, bringing the surround-sound speakers to life and change the music to something uplifting. A jazzy, upbeat band that I've never heard before fills the room. I crank it up loud, craving something different, some stimulation, then pad into the kitchen in my bare feet.

I open the door to the built-in wine cabinet that's always a cool fifty-two degrees and pick out a bottle of white wine. The label proudly announces it's called Naughty Girl Wine. Sounds perfect. After wrestling out the cork, I pour myself a large glass and sit down at the kitchen island to wait for my master's arrival home.

As absent as our physical contact has been, he dominates my days and nights. My schedule revolves around his. I'm all too aware of when he wakes and prepares for his workday, showering and moving about the room in the dim light, dropping his towel and dressing in the closet so as not to wake me. When he returns at night is the happiest time of my day. To prepare for his arrival, I shower, style my hair and apply makeup and greet him like I'm seeing a long lost friend. It's pathetic, but it's my life.

I sit and sip my wine, hoping the combination of the alcohol and the jazz music spilling from the speakers will lift my mood. My stomach rumbles loudly. *God, where is he?* I glance at the clock. He's later than usual. I pour myself another glass of wine and continue waiting. Dinner is ready and in the warming tray, as usual, and I can't help peeking to see what Beth's left us tonight. Its steamed fish garnished with fragrant orange slices, oven-roasted root vegetables and a side of creamy risotto. My mouth waters just looking at it and I steal a couple of vegetables off of each plate, being sure to keep the portions even, popping them into my mouth and chewing greedily like I'm breaking numerous international laws. The garlicky carrots and parsnips practically melt in my mouth and I steal another bite before replacing the covers on the two plates.

After two glasses of wine, I'm slightly buzzed and grab the remote for the sound system again. This cool jazz is giving me a headache. I flip absently through the music choices, not knowing what I'm searching for until I find it. Heart thumping, booty popping hip hop fills the room and my lips curl up in a lazy smile. I haven't listened to this since high school.

I take another fortifying gulp of my wine and

rise from the stool I'm slumped in, suddenly needing to move. I shimmy and shake across the kitchen, rolling my hips and lip-syncing along to the lyrics.

I dance while watching my reflection in the glass window across the room. Sticking my ass out, I give it a little shake. *How could he not want this?*

"What the hell are you doing?" Colton's deep voice rumbles behind me.

Gah! My hand flies to my heart and I spin around, my spine instantly straightening. I meet his eyes, taking in his amused expression. My face flames fire-engine red and my mouth opens uselessly, then closes again, knowing I've been busted.

Colton's dressed like he always is when he returns home from work. A custom tailored dark suit, light shirt and coordinating tie. Tonight the tie hangs loosely around his open shirt collar and his eyes are ringed with dark circles. He looks tired, but also amused. His mouth is lifted into a crooked smirk.

Making a split second decision, I saunter over to him, swaying to the beat of the still pumping music and grab his tie, tugging him closer. His body brushes against mine and the awareness of his broad muscular frame and captivating scent send endorphins skittering through my blood steam. Maybe it's the wine, maybe it's the music, or it could just be my lack of control in my new environment, but whatever the reason, I'm feeling bold. Alive for the first time in a long time. I drag a fingertip down the length of his tie, appreciating the feel of fine silk against my skin. Colton eyes my movements, but remains completely still as his breathing grows ragged.

Tired of being ignored, I grip his tie and work my hips back and forth in front of his lap, rolling my pelvis to the beat of the music, careful not to brush up against him, I'm just trying to show him there's more to me than the kept little girl he treats me as.

His amused grin falls away and his face takes on a more serious expression. His eyes drop from mine and slide lower, traveling slowly down my body. His look is ravenous and my pulse riots in my neck. The way his eyes are glued to my body is too much. The healthy dose of courage, courtesy of the half bottle of wine I'd consumed, all but evaporates, and my dancing comes to a halt.

His hand circles my waist, his thumb grazing back and forth across my hip bone. "I never took you for a Rhianna fan," he murmurs.

I merely nod and his hand falls away. I immediately notice its absence. Grabbing the remote, I tap the screen several times to bring the volume down to a more reasonable level.

"Naughty Girl, huh?" Colton asks, plucking the wine bottle from the counter. "Are you drunk, Sophie?" He sends me a questioning look and I lift one eyebrow. Why do I feel like a rebellious teenager who's broken into daddy's liquor cabinet?

He surprises me by bringing the bottle to his lips and taking a long swig. I watch the thick column of his throat as he swallows and little goosebumps break out across my belly. When he's done, he wipes his mouth with the back of his hand. "I've had a hell of a day." He grabs another bottle of wine and two fresh glasses. "Come on."

Dinner is all but forgotten. I have wine and Colton to keep me company and my boredom is temporarily at bay. *Hallelujah!*

I follow him through the house, into his darkened office and out onto the deck. As soon as he slides open the glass doors, the gentle whooshing sound of the ocean welcomes us. It instantly soothes me.

He strips off his suit jacket and removes the tie over his head, hanging both on the railing to the deck where they lightly flutter in the breeze. Colton sinks down into one of the lounge chairs and begins uncorking the bottle. I slide into the seat next to him and accept the glass of cool, crisp wine he passes me.

It's not as sweet as the bottle I'd opened, but subtle buttery flavors greet my palate. Mmm. I let out a tiny moan and Colton's eyes race over to mine.

"Care to tell me what tonight was all about?" he asks.

"What?" I play dumb.

"The club music, the wine, the dancing…" He lifts one dark eyebrow, his playful smirk is back.

"What was wrong with my dancing?"

Fighting off a smile, he clears his throat. "There wasn't a damn thing wrong with it, sweetness. You just surprise me, is all."

"It's boring here all day. I'm thinking about getting a job," I say, looking over at him to check his reaction.

"I've provided everything you could need.

Why would you want to work?" He seems surprised.

After paying for my sister's care, I still have several hundred thousand dollars in the bank. And I'm living expense-free. I should enjoy it, right? Only I can't. That's not me. I've never taken a hand-out in my life. "It's not about the money, I just need something to do. I can't lounge around all day with the only thing to do is go shopping with Marta using your credit cards. I want something for me. A purpose." Just saying it out loud renews my decision.

He takes another thoughtful sip of his wine, his full lips resting on the edge of the glass more distracting than it should be. "If that's what you want. What kind of job?" he asks.

"I don't know. Maybe at a coffee shop, or restocking books at the library. It doesn't matter. Just something that gets me out of the house."

"You're welcome to get a job, as long as you're home in the evenings when I am."

I nod. That sounds good to me too. I've come to enjoy his company at night. My boredom is isolated to the daytime hours. I didn't enjoy sitting alone in this too big house with too many thoughts running rampant through my head. It isn't healthy. "Thank you."

"What did you do today?" he asks, like he usually does.

"I read, went for a swim." I shrug and focus on my wine. I don't want to tell him that in the hours before he gets home, I shower and get myself ready, taking extra time to blow dry my hair and put on the dark colored lingerie that Marta insisted he'd like. It's like even my bras and panties are mocking me, whispering against my skin that he's not interested.

"What's wrong?" He lifts my chin to meet his concerned gaze. I guess he can read me better than I thought.

"Nothing." I straighten my shoulders, shaking the feelings away. There's no reason to feel rejected. If anything, I should be relieved. But if the situation were different—if I wasn't here under these pretenses, I'd still no doubt feel rejected by his lack of interest. He's a beautiful, charming, wealthy man. I guess it was dumb to believe that a man like him would be interested in someone like me. A dull, inexperienced virgin who dances in the kitchen to Rihanna.

His eyes hesitantly leave mine and though I can sense he wants to press the issue further, he closes his mouth and refills my wine glass.

"What happened at work today?" I recall him saying he'd had a rough day.

His eyes harden and he looks out at the dark blue water, growing quiet. It occurs to me that I don't really know what he does. He's very private about his business. "Nothing with work, it was actually something…personal that popped up unexpectedly. I need to go to New York and take care of it."

"New York? When?" Of course what I really want to know is what personal matter he could have in New York, since I know virtually nothing of his past.

He shrugs. "Soon. Maybe this weekend." His tone tells me its not something he wants to discuss, though I don't like the thought of him leaving.

I want to get back the flirty, playful attitude that seems to have faded with my complaints about boredom and whatever personal drama had Colton frowning out at the ocean.

"I have an idea," I announce, hopping up from my chair. "Stay here."

He nods, and watches me retreat through the glass door.

I jog upstairs and search through my toiletries until I find it.

I'm slightly winded when I make it back outside and Colton's eyes drop to see what I've gone to retrieve. I hold up the bottle of oil. "I thought you could use a little relaxation." I wave the massage oil temptingly in front of him and smile.

He eyes me curiously like he's trying to figure out my motives. It never occurred to me that he'd assume I was doing this out of obligation. It was a simple gesture—something nice you'd do for a friend, or a boyfriend when he'd had a trying day.

"Strip," I order, pointing to his dress shirt. I won't let him turn this into something weird.

He complies, watching me while he unbuttons and shrugs out of the shirt. Even though I should be used to seeing him in various states of undress by now, but each time, his masculine beauty hits me full force. His toned chest and chiseled abs look positively lickable in the glowing moonlight. *Focus, Sophie. Things aren't like that between you two*. I take a deep breath and motion for him to turn over and lay on his stomach. After dropping the shirt to the deck, he rolls on his lounger, lying flat for me.

Without thinking, I straddle him, sitting right on his butt and draping one leg on either side of his hips. "Am I too heavy?" I ask.

"You're fine," he says. He folds his arms under his chin, making his shoulder muscles bulge. He looks completely at peace and comfortable with my weight on top of him, so I decide to believe him.

Dripping some of the fragrant lavender scented oil into my hand, I rub my palms together to warm it before spreading it over his back. His frame is so broad that my small hands seem to barely make a dent in the expanse of canvas I want to cover. At first I think he's incredibly tense and I tell him to relax.

"I am," he mumbles.

And then I realize he's just rock hard with muscle. *Geez.* I splay my hands across his upper back, rubbing steadily. I'm unaccustomed to touching a man so intimately. His skin is smooth and lightly tanned and I love the feel of him under my hands. Warm and strong and powerful.

I rub my hands up his neck and into his hair,

massaging his scalp and he groans. I'm all too aware of how I'm sitting perched on top of him. My center is resting against his firm backside and the seam of my shorts pressing against my cleft. I squirm the tiniest bit, trying to adjust the way I'm sitting, but it only puts additional friction between my thighs. My clit begins to throb in time with my accelerating heartbeat. *Shit. I'm horny.* I blame it on too much wine, too much warm male perfection underneath me.

I rise to my feet, needing to separate myself from his tempting body. "Flip over," I tell him. I didn't get to rub his shoulders properly in that position. I straddle him once again, this time sitting across his thighs.

With Colton lying flat on his back, I massage his shoulders, then his firm biceps. His eyes slip closed, his mouth softens as a relaxed expression overtakes his face. I can ogle him properly in this position. And I do. From his handsome face, shadowed with a hint of dark stubble, to the thick column of his throat, down his smooth chest, the delectable grooves in his abs, to the trail of fine hair that disappears under his dress pants. He's beautiful, and very tempting.

Touching his solid arms is not helping my libido. If anything, my core heats up even more and I realize I'm becoming wet. I release a grunt of frustration and his eyes open and find mine. I realize my hands, seeming to have a mind of their own, are now rubbing his chest, brushing over his flat nipples and down further to trace his abs. He releases a soft hiss. My body floods with sexual awareness like nothing I've ever felt before. I'm desperate to feel his hands on my body too, to be consumed by the deep, hungry kisses I remember.

Colton watches me with dark eyes, his breathing shallow and rapid, much like mine.

Glancing down, I see his cock is half hard and rising the closer my hands get to his lap. My heart rate speeds up as this moment takes on a deeper meaning. I'm perched atop him, tending to him, and we're bathed in moonlight with the soft sound of waves lapping lazily behind us. It's perfect. Romantic, even.

Without pausing to think, I reach for his belt buckle and undo the stiff leather, my fingers trembling as I open his pants and ease down the zipper. His cock flexes beneath the confines of his black boxer briefs and I release a tiny whimper. I want to coat my hands in oil and slide them up and down his solid length, to hear him growl out my name and watch him lose all his perfect control and come all over his hard abs.

My panties are soaked and my heartbeat is pounding in all my pulse points. Just as my fingers dip inside his waistband to reach for his cock, he grabs my wrist and stops me.

"You don't have to do that." His voice is soft, but the hold on my wrist is firm.

I'm breathless and turned on and the harsh sting of rejection is like a slap to the face. It's totally unexpected and more brutal than ever imagined. He doesn't want me touching him. I rise to my feet on unsteady legs, Colton's eyes following my movements. The wine creates a sour pit in my stomach and my head is spinning. "Why did you bring me here?" I hate that my voice is too high and shaky. "I want the truth." I bite out the words and wait.

His eyes dart away from mine. "Companionship." He's holding something back. And I want to know what. I watch him for a second longer. He adjusts himself, tucking his huge erection back inside his pants and pulling up the zipper.

"What is this...this *arrangement*?" I toss my hands up in the air, frustrated, both sexually and emotionally beyond belief.

"Don't push me, Sophie."

My name on his lips is a warning, but I press on. "Just tell me you don't want me here. Send me away." I can see his desire for me as clear as day. I think he does want me, which makes him denying us both all the more confusing.

"There are things about my past you don't understand," he says, his tone low and calm, but his face holds an expression of silent agony.

"Then tell me. I'm sharing your home, your bed—I'm here for another five months. Are we really going to keep ignoring this?"

"Ignoring what?" he growls, his voice rough.

My gaze wanders to his lap and I unconsciously lick my lips. *Crap*.

If he's going to act like he's unaffected, then so am I. Pushing my legs into action, I rush inside, suddenly desperate to be away from him. I dart up the stairs, slamming the master bedroom door closed behind me.

This is the most confusing arrangement I've ever been part of. I might not have wanted a physical relationship when I first came here, but ever so slowly, Colton's gentle demeanor and quiet nature won me over. I want him to feel about me the way I do about him. I want to explore these new feelings of arousal bubbling up inside of me.

Tearing my shirt off my overheated skin, I drop it to the floor. After turning on the shower, I push down my shorts and panties, and step under the spray of the lukewarm shower.

Colton is an asshole. A sexy, yet evil man. I wasn't even asking for anything in return, I'd just wanted to touch him tonight, innocently at first, and then well, not-so-innocently, but even that was off-limits. It was a harsh wake-up call about my arrangement with this man. As I scrub my body under the warm water, I decide to move my things into one of the guest rooms. I don't care about his need for *companionship*.

As I finish washing myself, I realize I'm still much too overheated and turned on. My nipples are puckered tight and my body is begging for a release. I run one hand down my stomach, cupping the sensitive flesh between my legs and release a strangled groan. I rarely touch myself like this, feeling unsure and awkward about it most of the time. Tonight is not one of those times. I need this release like I need my next breath. Lowering my-self to the stone bench just out of the direct spray of water, I spread my legs and touch the slippery folds, surprised to feel how wet I still am.

My fingertips pick up speed, circling and rubbing my clit while dirty thoughts of Colton push into my mind. Rubbing my nipples with one hand while my other stimulates the firm nub at my center.

Sensing I'm no longer alone, my eyes fly open to discover Colton standing across from me, watching me pleasure myself through the glass shower wall. His eyes wander my naked body and I snap my legs together. The high I'd pushed my body toward comes barreling down, my orgasm vanishing before it has the chance to reach its peak.

Colton

Holy fuck.

The sight before me changes everything.

I'd assumed all along that Sophie didn't want me touching her. But after tonight when I'd stopped her and removed her hands from my lap, she'd come upstairs and was now pleasuring herself. All the breath leaves my lungs at once.

Pushing her away had been the hardest damn moment of my life. I didn't want her touching me out of some strange sense of obligation, or because she thought she owed me. But her flushed cheeks, and swollen pussy tell me instantly she hadn't been doing anything out of obligation. Sophie wanted me.

The realization rings like a gunshot in my ears. I can't think, can't see straight. All I can do is stare at her while my blood pumps out of control in my veins. She's enchanting and different, like an exotic animal I could observe for hours on end.

Before I can even process what I'm doing, my pants and boxers are around my ankles and I'm kicking them off. Stepping under the warm water, I offer her a hand and Sophie accepts, rising to her feet to stand before me completely nude and wet.

Goddamn.

The slick of her warm skin against mine is the best feeling in the world. We've been building toward this for too damn long. Living in the same close quarters, sharing a bed, dining together, all the while avoiding the sexual tension building between us. I'd thought it was one sided, but seeing the evidence of her arousal is too much. I'm hard as a fucking rock. I want to bury myself balls deep inside her sweet body and never let her go. Those are dangerous thoughts.

"You wanted me," I say, looking in her eyes.

She blinks up at me, her blue eyes softening.

"Say it," I command.

"I… I want you…" she breathes.

My mouth crashes against hers, our tongues tangling wildly. Damn, I'd forgotten how soft and lush her lips were. She tastes of wine and I devour every bit of her I can, my hands slipping down her curves to grip her ass and haul her closer. Running my hands over the round globes of flesh, Sophie tilts her hips, pressing her groin closer to mine. *Fuck.*

She wants this as badly as I do, which doesn't make our situation any easier or less confusing. It's a mind fuck. A battle I know I'm going to lose. I am a man pushed to my breaking point. I can't walk away. I won't leave Sophie to deal with the aftermath of my rejection. And that's what it had been. I'd been denying my want of her for weeks. I'd held myself back from taking something that wasn't mine. But tonight, when she'd reached for my belt, I realize now that had been her decision.

The spray of warm water hits my back, bringing me back into the moment. My blood is rushing in my ears and my heart is pounding. I want nothing more than to feel the heat of her soft curves molding to my chest and I pull her tighter against me.

The whisper of her hot breath rushing against my neck is more intimate than expected. Her body is pressed tightly to mine. She's giving herself to me. That knowledge is a potent thing, but I won't abuse my power. I pull a deep breath into my lungs and vow to go slow, to take my time. If she's letting me touch her, I will make damn sure this is good for her.

The press of her heavy breasts against my chest is too much to resist, I bring my hands up and cup her tits, unable to wait any longer. They're firm and soft at the same time and when my thumbs graze her nipples her breath shudders against my neck. I rub them back and forth, slowly, letting her get used to me touching her. Sensing she wants more, I give them a little tug and her whimper punctuates the silence beautifully.

"I want to watch you touch yourself," I breathe against her neck.

Her eyes perk up to mine and she chews on her

lower lip. I don't want her to feel embarrassed that I caught her. Shit, she caught me watching porn, preparing to jerk myself off the other night, even though neither of us spoke about it.

She doesn't respond, but I take her right hand in mine, the hand she'd been using to touch herself, and place it between her legs. A heavy sigh falls from her lips as I press her fingers into the rosebud of her clit. "Feel how swollen your clit is." I press our joined fingers harder against her. "Touch your pussy for me. Make it feel good," I whisper.

Her fingers begin to circle and her breath falters in her chest. I keep my hand on hers so that both of us are pleasuring her. I watch her eyes slip closed and a look of bliss overtakes her face. Breathless moans push past her lips as her pace builds. She's so incredibly worked up and ready, its sexy as hell.

I feel like a fucking fool for waiting. I'd assumed all these weeks, ever since I brought home the bottle of oil that she thought was lubricant, that she wouldn't welcome my touch. I'm not some sick, sadistic Dom that gets off on the thought of forcing a woman to submit. Knowing she wants this every bit as much as me changes everything. Well, almost everything. She is still a virgin, and I'm still… I push the thought away. I will deal with my past later. Nothing will spoil this moment with a wet, naked and willing Sophie in my arms.

Her eyes are wild, uninhibited like I've never seen before. I fucking love it. Her movements grow urgent. Desperate. Uneven breaths push past her lips. She's rubbing her clit in tiny circles, making me ache to take over, when all of a sudden her movements still and she releases a frustrated sigh.

My heartbeat slams to a stop. "What's wrong?"

"I can't…"

"You can't?" I repeat, voice little more than a harsh pant.

"I can't come without my vibrator," she whispers, her voice a hoarse plea and her mouth turned down in a pout.

The hell she can't. The alpha male inside me perks up his ears and beats on his chest. Suddenly watching her unravel is the only thing on my mind. "I've got you, sweetness." She'll come so hard she'll forget her own damn name.

She shakes her head. "I've tried…I get close, but…"

I meet her eyes. I don't need some damn toy to get her off, but if the safety net of a toy is more comfortable than having me touch her I have no problem going to retrieve it. "Where is it?"

"At home. I don't have it here."

Well that settles that. "You're telling me that you've never had an orgasm either on your own or with a partner?"

"There was only one partner before you and…" her voice trembles.

I hush her with the press of my lips to hers. Knowing I'm going to be the first man in so many ways makes all my blood rush south.

"How in the fuck did you learn to suck cock like that?"

Her cheeks grow rosy and she looks down at the marble floor between our bare feet.

"Answer me, sweetness." I tilt her chin up to mine.

Her eyelashes flutter against her cheeks as she struggles to make eye contact. "I might have watched a few porn videos before the auction, just to be sure I knew how."

Holy shit. Trained by porn stars, yet as pure and sweet as they come. I can't escape the growl of satisfaction that murmurs from my throat.

She bites down on her plump lower lip, causing my erection to strain as I imagine her mouth around my cock, and the feeling of the gentle tug of her teeth against my skin.

"Just relax and breathe for me, okay?"

She nods, her shoulders dropping just slightly as she inhales. "I've never…I've been close a few times. I think."

"Do you trust me?" I ask.

She blinks up at with solemn blue yes. "Yes."

I can tell she means it and I like that. A fuck of a lot.

"Just relax and let me make you feel good, okay?" She'd probably put so much damn pressure on herself, or worse, listened to some asshole ex who didn't know the clitoris from the g-spot and had psyched herself out. I had to believe there wasn't anything wrong with her anatomy. The trick would be to get her brain to quiet down so that her body could just relax and enjoy.

She draws another deep breath and some of the tension in her posture falls away.

"Can I touch you?" I whisper against the skin at her neck.

She nods enthusiastically. "God, yes."

I swallow the heavy lump in my throat. I'm scared that if I start touching her, I won't have the restraint to stop. But unable to keep myself from taking what I want, I slide my hand down her belly, finding her center slick and wet. It sends a jolt of desire straight to my dick, which leaps enthusiastically against her stomach.

With my thumb pressing firmly over her clit, my index finger slides against her tight opening and I feel her flinch. I want to penetrate her so badly I can taste it.

Sophie grips me at the same time I begin rubbing the outside of her opening, teasing her. She moves her hand up and down my shaft. Her tight grip is almost too much for me to handle. I've craved her touch for so long, it won't take me long to come undone.

"Easy baby, go slow," I remind her. I want to draw this out, and I won't last long if she keeps pumping my cock like that.

Sophie slows her pace, which allows some of the blood to flow back into my head, and I resume pleasuring her. Parting her folds, I find the swollen nub peeking out at me and using her own moisture, I caress her again and again. A breathy groan crawls up Sophie's chest and escapes past her parted lips. I touch her lightly, gently, taking my time and getting to know what she likes. Her body trembles against mine as she fights to remain standing.

Locking one arm around her waist, I continue my assault. My mouth moves to her breasts and I lick one nipple and then the other.

I press my finger forward. She's slippery and soaking wet, and even though she's as tight as a glove, my finger slides in easily. A ragged moan tangles in her throat and my lips crash down on hers.

I drag my finger in and out of her molten heat and feel her flex around my knuckle. "You want me to fuck this tight little opening?" Her groan of desperation is too much. I can't even let myself think about how good she'll feel around my cock, or I'll come too fast and embarrass myself.

She inhales sharply and watches me while I slowly but carefully add a second finger. Her body grips me and her eyes slip closed as a little whimper falls from her mouth.

I curl my fingers upward and press down on her clit. She cries out, her body quaking in my arms as she comes. The sight of her coming on my hand pushes me over the edge, and a hot stream of semen spurts to the tile floor between us, marking Sophie's belly in the process. I growl out my release, burying my face in her neck and biting down softly to keep from moaning.

"*Fuck.*"

When I look up, she's smiling at me. Her blue eyes dance on mine and her face is pink. She looks happy—completely and utterly happy and satisfied. Even though I love it, it makes me feel like an even bigger ass for denying her touch for so long. My mouth captures hers again and I kiss her hungrily, taking my time to explore every inch of her tongue with mine.

Once we both come down from the high of our climaxes, I realize the water has cooled around us. I crank up the hot water and wash Sophie's supple skin using a bottle of body wash from the shelf. She relaxes into my touch, letting me rub her shoulders, down her back and even between her legs. Her eyes find mine and we share a silent understanding. Even though our circumstances are anything but normal, I can tell this is our new normal. It's what we're both choosing. It scares me to think how compatible we are.

I'd been trying like hell to hold her at a distance, to keep her separate from my personal life — but there's no denying it, she's all I think about. She's all I want. Though it's entirely honest, the realization scares me. And it feels nice to be touched. Even if it's not real.

CHAPTER ELEVEN

Sophie

We're lying in bed, facing each other in the pale moonlight. I should feel self-conscious about our shower activities earlier, but all I feel is blissfully happy and relaxed. Knowing Colton wanted me just as badly as I wanted him—that his desire for me had nothing to do with the transaction at the auction and was the culmination of raw lust—made it that much better.

"I have an idea…" Colton says, looking at me thoughtfully. "About you working."

He's changed his mind. He doesn't want me out of the house, which was my sole purpose for wanting to find a job. I swallow heavily and meet his gaze. "What is it?"

His thumb reaches out to smooth the crinkle etched into my forehead. "How would you feel about working for one of my companies?"

It's just another way I'll be tied to him. I'd wanted something for me. But as I open my mouth to speak, he continues.

"It'd be for my charity organization. I'm sponsoring a huge project in Africa and could use an extra set of hands. Mostly office work — if you're good with word processing and filing. Kylie's my only full-time office employee, and she's been working seven days a week just trying to keep up with the workload. It'd actually be a huge help."

Knowing it's for charity, and that's he's not just throwing me some pity busy-work, I find myself nodding my head. "Okay. I'll do it."

"Perfect. I'll let Kylie know. You can start whenever it suits you."

"Tomorrow will be fine." I don't think I need another day of lounging in the sun or jogging aimlessly through Colton's winding neighborhood of mansions.

He chuckles. "Tomorrow it is."

Colton wakes me in the morning with tender kisses to the back of my neck and I push my bottom into his groin and moan at the dual sensations. The damp sucking kisses and the rigid length of his erection nestled between my cheeks perk me up instantly. I'm wide awake. And suddenly very much in the mood, remembering that earth-shattering orgasm he delivered last night.

He nips at the base of my neck, moving lower down my spine. "Does that feel nice, sweetness?"

"Yes," I breathe. Rolling over so I can see him, I bring my arms around his neck and snuggle closer. I like our new lack of boundaries when it comes to touching. It feels nice to be held after not having a man in my life for so long. Last night bonded us and it's obvious we're growing closer. I have a feeling I'm going to miss him even more than before when he's at work.

We kiss for several minutes and cuddle in the big, warm bed before Colton crawls out, saying he needs to shower and get ready for work. I guess I do too.

CHAPTER TWELVE

Sophie

Kylie is adorable. Probably a couple years older than me, she has wavy auburn hair tied in a messy bun on top of her head, and no makeup, but *geez*, she doesn't need it. Her cheeks are rosy pink and her green eyes are large and wide-set. She's barefoot and dressed in yoga pants and a tank top. "Hi!" She smiles widely, showing off perfectly straight white teeth. Does everyone in LA have teeth like this? "Don't just stand there, come in." She tugs me by the arm inside her front door, closing it behind me.

"I'm…"

"Sophie. I know. Colton is an absolute angel to send you. God, I was giddy when he called this morning." She leads me further into her house.

"Sorry about the mess." She waves in the direction of the disheveled living room and kitchen. "I'm a terrible housekeeper. Hope that's not a problem."

"No, it's fine." I navigate the little living room, dodging laundry baskets and stray toys as I follow her.

Kylie leads me out the backdoor and to a set of steps. "Office is up there." She points. "Go ahead, I'm just going to grab the baby monitor."

I start up the stairs, wondering what I'm getting myself into. Joining me a few seconds later, she explains that when Colton hired her to run the day to day operations of his charity, he built her a home office above her garage. Her tiny two-bedroom house didn't have any extra room to spare and she didn't want to have to put her baby in childcare. It was the perfect arrangement — and awfully generous of him. I want to ask how they know each other, but I keep my trap shut and my jealousy in check. I'm here to work.

We enter a roomy loft above the garage. There are plenty of big windows to let in the light, and two large work stations with laptops and filing cabinets spilling over with papers.

Kylie thrusts her arms out proudly. "Welcome

to the world headquarters of Highpoint Associates." She picks up a bottle and a baby rattle from the desk. "Seriously. Sorry about this. I would have cleaned up if I'd known you were coming."

"Trust me, its fine. I'm just happy to have a change of scenery. I've been cooped up at Colton's for weeks and I've been going a bit stir crazy."

"Wow. You live with him? That's…that's… huge…" She turns to me, her mouth hanging open in surprise. "And that house is freakin' incredible."

Interesting. She's been inside his home and seems to understand that him having a woman living with him is a big step. I find it both fascinating and utterly frustrating that Marta and now Kylie seem to possess intimate knowledge about Colton. He must not be as discreet as his seems with his affections. His restraint is only reserved for me. Of course I have no way of knowing if Kylie has actually slept with him, but the faraway look in her eyes tells me she's daydreaming of some memorable encounter with him. Oddly, it makes me want to hit something.

I shrug it off. "So, what's on the docket today?"

"Right." She gives her head a shake, pushing away the thought. "First I'm going to give you an overview of the work we've done so far, and then I'll explain what I'm hoping to accomplish next. You can be involved in any part of it that sounds interesting to you."

I nod. "Sounds good."

I listen while she explains, in more detail than Colton provided, about their mission to create a stable self-sustaining community in a sub-Saharan part of rural Africa. His vision is much more complex than just to provide clothing, food and medicine to people in need, like he'd humbly led me to believe. He wanted to do something bigger — something the residents could sustain long after he and his generous donations were gone. It's quite a bit more sophisticated than I ever imagined and I'm impressed. No wonder he's so busy.

He has a team of city planners, architects, engineers, teachers and doctors who are working together to drill for fresh, clean drinking water, plant crops and teach the local people about agriculture and farming as well as building a school for the children to ensure the next generation is prepared to lead. What Kylie is describing is a massive undertaking. He's essentially creating an entire community from the ground up. I get goosebumps listening to her speak and I'm suddenly really glad I didn't find a job at a coffee shop — this is much more worthwhile to devote my time to.

At the end of her explanation, Kylie provides an overview of the pertinent files on the laptop I'll be using. "I'm so glad you're here." She grins widely at me, showing off twin-dimples that make her look younger. "God, Stella was crazypants." Just then the baby monitor squawks and she jumps up from her seat. "Be right back."

She leaves me to work on creating mailing labels and to type up a letter to the additional investors Colton's secured. My head is spinning and the work is a needed distraction.

CHAPTER THIRTEEN

Sophie

After our erotic shower encounter, my relationship with Colton takes on a new meaning, changing in a subtle, but noticeable way. He texts me during the day while he's at work and calls once he's on his way home.

I've been working several days a week with Kylie, driving myself to her suburban home in one of Colton's cars. It's nice to feel like I'm making a contribution to something, and now that Colton and I are actually clicking, I feel a lot better about my situation.

He called at lunchtime today, sounding melancholy, which is completely out of character for him. I'd pressed him about what was wrong and he just said that it was a tough day and that he was looking forward to coming home.

At six o'clock, the house staff has been gone for hours and I'm anxiously awaiting his call to tell me he's on his way home. I can't wait to surprise him.

Finally my cell phone rings and I prance across the kitchen to retrieve it from the island. "Hello?"

"I'm on my way," he says, his voice flat and emotionless.

"Okay," I squeak. It will be my mission to cheer him up once he arrives.

When Colton arrives home thirty minutes later, I'm ready for him. I took special care getting ready too, taking an extra-long soak in the tub and shaving nearly every square inch of my body, and then prepared a special meal for him. It was the only thing I could think to do when I learned he was having a bad day, it's the same thing my mom used to make me when I needed comforting.

I meet him by the back door. His suit is rumpled and his expression is sour. When his gaze lifts to mine, his face softens, but I can see something is weighing on him and the need to help bubbles up inside of me.

"Did something happen at work?" I ask, helping him out of his jacket.

He tosses the garment onto the waiting bench. He does this every night and they miraculously end up freshly laundered and back in his closet. I don't even think he realizes it.

"Sort of," he says without meeting my eyes.

"I'm good listener. You can tell me things, you know? You can trust me," I assure him.

"I know. But when I get home, talking about my day is usually the last thing I want to do."

I nod. I know the feeling well. When Becca was sick, friends would encourage me to talk about it, and even though I appreciated the gesture, I knew talking about it would only bring all my worries and fears to the surface. Best to keep them locked away. So while I understood him, it made me even more curious about what could be troubling him.

"I made you dinner," I say.

"You cooked?" he asks, his voice lifting in uncertainty.

I nod my head, feeling insecure for some strange reason. It could be the curious way he's looking at me.

"What about Beth?"

"I sent her home." I have no authority to release his staff, but Colton doesn't say anything else, he just follows me into the kitchen, tugging at his tie to loosen it.

Now that he's here in the kitchen with me, I'm fidgety. Using two pot holders, I bring the dish I've prepared to the kitchen island and set it down in front of him. I feel like I'm showing off an elementary school science experiment. One with very questionable results.

He looks down at it curiously before meeting my eyes. "You made me mac-n-cheese?" He grins unevenly.

I instantly feel like a fool. This man has an entire staff of servants and a personal chef. He dines on things like organic beet and arugula salad, grilled swordfish and hand fed prawns. And I just made him elbow macaroni smothered in processed American cheese. His amused expression makes me want to crawl into a hole and die.

Why did I even bother? And now I feel particularly stupid, because I've sent his cook home for the night. "Nevermind." I grab the casserole dish to clear it away and his hand on my wrist stops me.

"Stop."

"It was a stupid effort." Wasted.

"Stop," he says again, removing my hands from the dish. "You cooked for me." My eyes jerk up to his, trying to make sense of the reverence in his words. "I haven't had a home cooked meal like this—comfort food—in…a long damn time. Thank you."

I'd misread his reaction. He's surprised. And apparently happy. Pulling out a stool at the island, he sits down and helps himself to a heaping portion, piling a mound of macaroni in his bowl without pretense. "Do we have any milk?" he asks around a big mouthful of pasta.

I laugh at him and head to the massive fridge, and pull out a carton of organic milk to pour him a glass. I watch Colton eat two big servings of the dish, and he insists I join him. We sit side by side at the countertop, stuffing ourselves with ooey-gooey melted cheese and pasta. It actually tastes halfway decent and I'm relieved. Though if I'm being honest, it's his reaction that makes my heart soar.

He's instantly more light-hearted and seems to have let whatever stress was troubling him slip away.

"How are things going with Kylie? She says you're a godsend."

"It's fine. Kylie's a sweet girl and it's exactly what I wanted—something to get me out of the house."

"Good." Colton digs in for another bite, seemingly satisfied with my response.

"More milk?" I ask, noticing his glass is almost empty.

He looks at it thoughtfully for a second. "Actually...which wine pairs well with mac-n-cheese? Pinot Grigio?"

I nod. "Sure. If you like." I make a move to get up and his hand on my elbow stops me.

"Stay put. I'll get it."

I glance down at the casserole dish that we've made a rather impressive dent in, and cover it with the lid, before setting it inside the fridge.

He returns a moment later with two glasses of wine and hands me one. "Thank you for this," he says, his voice solemn and his eyes on mine.

I nod and meet his gaze, taking a sip of wine. *Mmm.* Colton Drake, wine and yummy comfort food. My day is complete.

We set our bowls in the sink and head outside to the balcony off his office, settling into the lounge chairs to sip our wine. After several minutes the wine and soundtrack of the waves relaxes me.

"What should we do now?" The sultry tone to my voice is entirely unintended, but his dark gaze finds mine and my sex muscles tighten. *Eep!* The hungry look in his eyes is new and unnerving.

"Come here."

I slide off my seat and cross the few steps until I'm standing directly before him. My heart hammers unevenly in my chest and the sensuous look in his eyes has me wondering if tonight is *the night*. Though I'd been merely curious before, I'm now dying to know what it will feel like when he finally takes me. As strange as it sounds, it's an invasion I would welcome. To be wrapped up in his strong arms, to feel his full lips on mine and to finally understand what all the fuss over sex is about…I shudder at the thought.

"Are you cold?" Colton's fingertips reach out to stroke my upper arms.

I shake my head. The shivers racing along my skin have nothing to do with the temperature.

"What happened the other night…" he pauses, his tongue lazily stroking his bottom lip as his eyes burn on mine, "was that okay with you?"

I swallow the massive lump in my throat. I should have felt horribly embarrassed that he'd caught me masturbating in his shower. Yet any and all feelings of shame are absent. I feel liberated, free. And his response, to strip down and join me, his hard cock tall and proud pressing into my skin showed me that he felt the exact same way. There was something deeply comforting about that. And knowing that he knew how to pleasure my body better than I did? That was the icing on a pretty freaking awesome cake.

"Y-yes," I answer, blinking up at him.

He reaches up to trace my bottom lip with his thumb and then hooks his palm around the back of my neck, drawing my mouth closer to his. "Good girl." He leans in closer, wrapping his hands around the backs of my bare knees. "Take off your panties," he whispers.

"Here?" The balcony is private, but we're still outside.

He doesn't respond, his eyes just stay locked on mine. Clearly there's no room for negotiation.

I'm wearing one of the cute sundresses I'd bought with Marta my first week here, and the cool night air nips at me as I reach under my dress and slide the panties down my legs. They drop to my ankles and I step out of them, handing the scrap of navy silk to him with a cheeky grin.

I have no idea what he wants, but his hand glides up my inner thigh, pushing my dress up out of the way. His fingers caress my bare skin. Even after the bikini wax started to grow out, I've kept myself shaved smooth, liking how sensual it makes me feel.

His eyes find mine as he continues lightly rubbing me. I can feel myself getting wet as endorphins rush into my blood steam. I wonder if last time was a fluke, or if I'll be able to reach climax again. God, I want to. I tilt my hips closer allowing him a better angle and Colton's mouth twitches with a smile.

"Come here." He takes my hand and helps me lower myself down onto his lap so I'm straddling him. My legs are spread wide and my bare pussy is close enough that he reaches down and begins rubbing me once again. His other hand curls around the back of my neck and he brings my mouth to his. His lips are soft and full and demanding.

He quickly takes charge of the kiss, his tongue caressing mine in a hypnotic rhythm. My entire body responds, my hips rocking closer and my hands pushing into his hair.

Reading my body's reactions, Colton picks up his pace, circling and rubbing my clit until I'm soaking wet and right on the edge of climax. The need to touch him spikes within me. I reach between us, unbuckling his belt and nearly rip his pants open in my mission. Once his thick, warm cock is in my hands he lets out a soft growling sound of pleasure. I pump my fist up and down, loving the way his desperate kisses feel as we move toward release together.

Gripping my ass underneath my dress, he tugs me closer until his hot length is nestled right up against my cleft. Angling my hips closer, I rock against him. His fingers bite into my skin he breaks the kiss, his eyes flashing dangerously on mine.

I slid up and down his cock, my slick skin so sensitive I can feel every hard ridge and vein as I ride him. I wonder what he would feel like inside…

"Careful," he growls, his voice sticking in his throat. His eyes are dark and half-closed like he's drowning in pleasure. I love it.

Ignoring his warning, I lift and lower myself on him, unable to stop moving against him. The friction of his solid cock against my sensitive clit is too much. Little cries of pleasure break the silence and I move faster, rubbing against his hard cock, chasing the orgasm I want so badly.

Colton watches me move against him, his hands still gripping my ass as I work my body against his. He feels so good. I wonder what it would feel like to let him finally push inside me... My body clenches and I cry out his name, coming in a wet gush all over him.

When the blur of my earth-shattering orgasm wears off, I open my eyes and meet his. His jaw is clenched tight and he looks angry.

"I'm...I'm sorry." I hop up from his lap and scramble away, afraid I've done something wrong.

CHAPTER FOURTEEN

Colton

I catch a hold of Sophie's wrist in my office and spin her to face me. Her cheeks are flushed and she's breathing rapidly, still trying to recover from her orgasm. She did not get to tease me, ride my dick until she came and then just disappear. There's nothing hotter than a confident girl who takes what she wants, but that is not how this works.

"I don't think so, sweetness," I growl.

She pulls her lower lip into her mouth and sucks. My cock pulses, reminding me of his predicament. He's still coated in her damp juices and now I want to watch her drop to her knees and lick them off. "Do you understand how close I was? How easily I could have lifted you up and pushed my way inside your hot little cunt?"

She lets out a squeak of surprise.

I reach under her dress and push two fingers inside her silky channel. Her eyes widen and latch onto mine as I pump my fingers in and out. "And it's my job to make sure this tight little pussy's ready for me. Isn't it?" I withdraw my fingers and reach down, gripping my cock and using her moisture to stroke him up and down. "Answer me."

"Y-yes," she stumbles, gazing down at the show I'm giving her.

"I could have hurt you. Made you bleed. We don't want that, now do we?"

She doesn't answer. Her blue eyes just blaze back at mine in a silent challenge.

The fuck?

My balls ache with the need to be inside her, but I can't. I won't until I've settled my past with Stella. The closer I grow to Sophie, the more I understand about her, I don't want to hurt her. I bought her as a way to have some fun and blow off steam, but somewhere along the way, it's become something more. Right from that very first morning when Pace looked her over with rapt interest, I became invested. In her. In us.

"The answer is no, Sophie. I don't want to hurt you." I force the words out of my mouth.

She draws a shuddering breath. "Isn't a sex slave supposed to, I don't know, actually have sex with her master?"

The desire to take her is a physical ache, but I force myself to remain composed. "That eager, huh?" I trail a damp fingertip along her lower lip and feel her inhale sharply.

"You bought me, expecting something in return. Call me crazy, but I thought that was how this worked," she challenges.

"Let's get one thing straight. I don't want a sex slave. I want a companion. A mistress. Call me conservative, but I don't like the term slave." I've paid Sophie to be here—she's not held captive against her will.

"A mistress?" she asks, raising an eyebrow at me.

"It suits you. You're my dirty little secret— a kept woman," I remind her, smoothing a hand along her backside, watching her pulse kick up in her neck. I couldn't have her questioning my motives. They was too fucked up for even me to think about, let alone admit to her. And since I wasn't willing to let Stella fuck up yet another thing in my life, I planned to handle her, and then I would make Sophie mine.

"Take off your dress."

She's still watching me jerk myself, so it takes her a minute to respond — her eyes snapping up to mine and her hands moving to lift the dress off over her head.

She's wearing the pale blue lace bra I remember from the first night and wordlessly, she unsnaps it and lets it fall to the floor.

I look down at my cock in my hand and then back at her mouth. Sophie gracefully drops to her knees between my feet and eagerly brings her mouth to me.

Fuuck.

The sweet warmth of her mouth as she licks the tip of my dick sends a bolt of pleasure ricocheting through me. I clench my abdominals and thread my fingers in her hair, forcing more of myself in between her lips. With her eyes looking up at mine, she takes me deeper, letting me control the pace as I thrust into her mouth. I push my hips forward in a lazy pace, wanting to draw this out as long as possible. She cups my balls, massaging them and I grunt in surprise when she gives them a little tug. *Shit.* This girl is good.

"Stroke me," I breathe, and Sophie obeys, wrapping one hand around my base and pumping in time with her bobbing mouth. Her rhythm is perfect. My shaft glistens with her saliva and the dual sensations are enough to send me spiraling over the edge way too soon and I brace one hand on my desk as my muscles tense.

"Soph..." I whisper a weak warning. She sucks me harder, hollowing out her cheeks, and my head drops back toward my shoulders as I empty myself into her.

She swallows every drop, like a goddamn champ, and I can't resist leaning down to kiss her skilled mouth. "That was fucking amazing."

"Glad you liked it."

I help her to her feet and kiss her neck, her chin, the tip of her nose. "Understatement."

She curls into me and I hold her. Close physical contact is something I've missed out on. Stella was never warm and snuggly and I'd lost my mom when I was twelve. It sounds lame, but I craved the tender feel, and the warmth of a soft female body. Intimacy in the most basic sense of the word has been missing from my life for a long damn time. It feels nice just to hold her close.

"You cooked for me," I murmur against her throat, as the start to our evening comes back to me.

"I was trying to help," she whispers.

The sense of falling overwhelms me and I cling to her more, wrapping her tightly in my arms. "Thank you for the macaroni." I kiss her temple, knowing I'm in deep shit.

Sophie

After washing my face and brushing my teeth, I saunter toward the bed wearing only a pair of panties. Call me crazy, but there's something I love about knowing that I tempt him, but he won't act on it yet, for whatever reason.

But rather than watching me from the bed, like I expected, Colton's staring down at his phone.

He's frowning. And considering how hard I just

made him come, I'm clueless about his foul mood.

"What's wrong?" I ask, crawling up onto the big bed beside him.

He sets down his phone and his eyes lift to mine. "One of my stocks is tanking," he says.

He's lying. He wasn't checking his stock performance. Before the screen went dark on his smart phone, I could see that he was texting with someone, his fingers flying over the keys as anger boiled up inside of him.

I let it go. Whoever it was, it's not something he wants to talk about with me, and considering the progress we're making, I don't want to ruin it. Of course I'm undeniably curious about his past, but for now, I have to accept the pieces of himself he's willing to share.

CHAPTER FIFTEEN

Colton

"I need to go to New York to take care of some things," I say to Pace in between reps.

I move away from the bench and wipe my brow with my towel. Pace takes a seat, gripping the bar with a confused look on his face. "Tell me this has nothing to do with seeing Stella."

"We both know I need to take care of this mess between us. This has dragged on way too fucking long."

"It's a bad idea, Colton. You never had any restraint where she was concerned. I just don't want to see you dragged back into something you worked so hard to untangle yourself from."

He's wrong about one thing — I've never untangled myself. "That's what this trip is about, I promise you that. Closure. Once and for all."

He lays back and I hand him the bench press bar. He pumps out fifteen reps, puffing out slow, even breaths. "And how many times over the past year have I heard that?"

He's right. I had let her get to me, to suck me back in, but this time felt different. This time I have Sophie in my life. It might not be much, but I have something on the horizon with a beautiful, sweet girl. And my damn moral compass won't let me pursue her the way I want until I'm free of the mega-beast.

We move onto squats, but he's still eyeing me curiously. "Are you taking Sophie with?"

"Fuck no. She doesn't know anything about me and Stella, and I prefer it that way. I was actually going to ask if you'd stop over, keep an eye on her."

"Don't trust her alone in your house, huh?"

"No, nothing like that. I just don't want her to get bored." She's working with Kylie now, but I know from experience evenings can be hard all alone in that big house.

"You got it, boss." Pace grins at me, a goofy smile that instantly tells me all the ways he plans to entertain her. It makes me want to pummel him. Christ, I need to get my head on straight.

CHAPTER SIXTEEN

Sophie

He hasn't mentioned going to New York again and I'd almost forgotten about it. But when we reach his bedroom that evening, he heads straight into the closet, grabs a leather duffle bag from a drawer and begins stuffing articles of clothing inside.

"Are you packing?" I ask, entering the room behind him.

My side of the closet has filled out nicely with new dresses, jeans and tops. That one lone camisole still hangs haphazardly from a hanger and I still wonder about its owner.

"Yeah. I can't put off going to New York any longer. I leave in the morning."

I nod, wondering if he'll ask me to go along, but he doesn't.

"It's just one night," he says, reading my mind. "And I've asked Pace to come over and check on you."

"Okay," I murmur. An entire day and night without the promise of hanging out with Colton to look forward to? I'll go stir crazy in this big house all alone, even with Pace stopping by. A plan takes shape in my brain. "I think I'll call Marta for a girls night." I saunter away, leaving Colton in his closet staring after me with his mouth hanging open.

"Are you a candle? Because I want to blow you." I purse my lips and blow. Marta chokes on her wine, sputtering loudly.

We're drunk and practicing pick-up lines to use on guys. After our second bottle of wine, the conversation took a turn for the dirty — beginning with Marta complaining about her lack of sex life.

"Oh! I've got one!" She rises to her unsteady feet and thrusts out her chest. "If I told you I worked for the post office, would you let me touch your package?"

I burst into a fit of giggles. She's smiling so big, I don't want to tell her it's the worst pick up line ever. "It could work." I nod.

She plops down on the couch beside me and grabs the bottle to pour herself more wine. Quirking an eyebrow my way, she thrusts the bottle at me. "Want some?"

Peering down into my half-full glass, I shake my head. I better pace myself. It's only eight o'clock and I'm decidedly buzzed.

"Seriously, why is it so hard to meet men in Los Angeles?" she complains, tucking her legs underneath her.

I shrug. "You're gorgeous, you can't seriously have problems meeting a guy."

Her gaze locks onto mine. "What about you?"

"What about me?"

"You and Colton. What's the real story?" She wiggles her eyebrows.

I chuckle nervously. "Nothing. No story." My heart beat kicks up at the mere mention of his name.

She rolls her eyes. "Liar. Are you guys, like together?"

I shake my head. I don't think so. I don't know how to classify us. Our precarious start has led to something more, only I have no idea what. On my end, real feelings are developing. He's driven, generous, utterly sexy and considerate. Of course I'm falling for him. But his own feelings remain tightly locked away. For all I know, he could be seeing someone else on the side. Although, I don't know when he'd have the time. In between work, working out and me, he doesn't have any free time.

Her eyes are still on me, weighing my reaction. "There's not much to tell. Honestly, I have no idea how he feels about me."

"Have you slept with him?" she asks, her voice dropping lower.

*Have yo*u? I want to ask.

"No," I admit.

She bites her lip. "Hmm. That's interesting."

I want to ask her what's so interesting about it, but instead I decide to pour myself more wine after all. The doorbell chimes and Marta hops up from her perch on the sofa.

"I'll get it!"

Moments later, Marta strolls back into the den with Pace trailing behind her. "Look who I found."

I'd forgotten that Colton said he'd send Pace over to check on me. Pace eyes the coffee table where the wine bottles signal exactly what we've been up to.

"Join us?" I grin at him.

He lifts two empty bottles from the table and flashes me a naughty smirk. "Trouble."

"Who, us?" Marta bats her eyelashes at him.

"I'm good, thanks though. I just came to check on you ladies, make sure you're not getting into too much mischief while the boss is away."

"We're being good. We're just discussing why meeting a good man is so hard. Seriously, what's a girl gotta do to get laid in this town?" Marta complains, taking another sip of wine.

Amusement gleams in Pace's eyes and his lips curl into one of his delicious trademark smiles. "Let me know if I can help."

Marta rolls her eyes. "Colton would have your balls if you touched me and we both know it."

Pace's smile fades. "True enough."

I wonder what that's all about, but my tummy grumbles, reminding me that we'd foregone dinner in favor of alcohol. I head to the kitchen, grabbing handfuls of crackers and pretzels and munching on them as I head back to the den where Pace and Marta are speaking in low, hushed tones. I sense the mood of the evening has shifted, only I have no idea why.

"He's an asshole if he keeps this from her," Marta says.

"He's trying to figure it out, so we need to cut him some slack and let him do this his way," Pace reminds her, his voice firm.

My crunching attracts their attention and the conversation immediately stops. "Are you guys talking about Colton?" I ask, swallowing down a dry mouthful of crackers. It's obvious that they were, I just want to see if they'll be honest or try to lie to me.

They exchange a silent look.

I plop down on the sofa across from them, meeting Pace's concerned gaze. "Why doesn't he like me?" The words fall from my mouth before I can filter them. Maybe I've had more wine than I realized.

"I know he likes you," Pace says, confidence seeping from his every word.

"How?" I blurt.

"Because he's finally dealing with shit he should have years ago."

"Pace…" Marta warns.

"Relax. I'm not going to spill the beans. Besides, you know I'm right," he says.

I wish I hadn't drunk so much, I wish my head was clear enough to put together the puzzle pieces forming before me.

"Come on, we're going out. Operation mancandy is going into effect starting tonight—for both of us," Marta announces, hoping up from the couch. "Pace you'll take us out clubbing, won't you?"

He frowns but nods his head. "I'll make sure you're safe."

I follow Marta upstairs to Colton's bedroom. She heads straight for the closet and begins picking out outfits for both of us. It's been a long, long time since I've been out, but this is what people my age do, right?

Marta changes into a denim mini skirt and halter top right in the closet. Knowing Pace is in the other room, sitting on the chaise, I'll take my black shift dress to the bathroom to change. I haven't had *that* much wine.

Marta saunters toward the bed and plops down. "God, I'd forgotten how comfortable this bed is. Holy shit." She snuggles into the pillows. "It's like heaven threw up and this bed is the result."

I want to ask her when the hell she's been in his bed, but I don't. I might belong to him, but he's not mine. And I don't want to imagine anyone besides me in his bed. Needing to hide my warring emotions, I head into the bathroom to get ready.

In the mirror, I see a girl with wide, curious blue eyes and her heart wide open. It's a dangerous combination. Falling for the man who bought me was never part of the deal. Could I be any more naïve? He hasn't even slept with me yet, and already my feelings are running way too deep. A tiny thought pushes into my brain. *Maybe he hasn't slept with you yet because he actually likes you.*

Unwilling to let myself get carried away with the thought, I change into the dress, leaving my clothes in a heap on the bathroom floor, then fluff my flat brown hair in the mirror. My cheeks are flushed pink from the wine, but my lips look pale in comparison. I wonder if Marta has some lip gloss I can borrow.

"Marta?" I exit the bathroom only to find her stretched out across the bed sound asleep.

Pace looks up at me from the chaise. "I think she's out for the night."

Marta lets out a soft snore and curls onto her side.

I shrug. "That's fine." I'd be just as happy changing into pjs and curling up with the TV remote.

"Thanks for coming tonight," I say to Pace.

"Not a problem." He rises to his feet. "The truth is, I wanted to come over and check on you. I was getting worried about you. Colton keeps you locked away like some sex slave."

My cheeks go bright red, but I force a laugh from my lips. Pace doesn't know — he couldn't possibly, I remind myself. "I'm doing good. You don't have to worry."

"He likes you, you know."

I nod. I want to believe that. It's crazy how much I can miss him. The house is too big and feels lifeless and empty without his presence.

I move to walk Pace out, but he stops me.

"I can lock up."

"Thanks."

Just before he reaches the bedroom door, he turns back to face me. "Just so you know, he would never cheat. He falls hard, gives people way too many chances and is kind and generous to a fault. Be careful with him."

I strip out of the dress with Pace's strange warning still ringing in my ears. I throw on one of Colton's t-shirts. Now that I've grown used to sleeping with him, with his warm arms around me, tonight I'll have to settle for his scent.

Luckily the bed is big enough that I hardly notice Marta curled up on the opposite end.

I'm drifting off to sleep when my cell phone pings, informing me of a new text.

Colton: Are you awake?

My mouth curls into a happy grin and I hit call rather than reply to his text, eager to hear his deep, rumbly voice. I burrow myself under the covers so as not to wake Marta.

"Hello?"

"Hi," I return.

"Hi, sweetness. How was your girl's night?"

Hearing the nickname reserved just for me and his gruff voice soothes me more than I could have imagined. I look over at Marta's sleeping form in the bed next to me. "It was fun. How is…everything going there?"

"Eh. It's to be expected, but I hope to have all this figured out soon so I can put it behind me."

I hate the not knowing. "Will you tell me…"

"Not yet. Just trust me, okay?"

I nod, before realizing he can't see me. "Okay." The crazy thing is, I do trust him. So far, he's given me no reason not to. And while I'm terrified that I'll end up hurt and alone at the end of this…I can't help myself. I'm feeling things I have no right to feel. "Will you be home tomorrow?"

"I have to stay another day," he says, his voice somber.

Oh. Tomorrow is Sunday. What business could he possibly have on Sunday? "Is it work or personal?"

"Sophie…" He lets out a soft groan. "I wish I could explain it all to you, but I don't want you to hate me."

"I could never hate you."

"You promise?"

I yawn, unable to hold it in a second longer. "Uh huh."

He chuckles, sending little vibrating tingles all through me. "Get some sleep, sweet girl. I'll see you on Monday."

"Okay." I nestle into the pillow, hating that I have to wait another day to feel his strong arms around me.

CHAPTER SEVENTEEN

Colton

The trip was a complete bust. I'd wasted the last several years of my life on someone who I now realize was never worth my time, and one weekend in her presence hadn't fixed a damn thing. I don't know why I'd thought it would.

With a woman like Sophie in my life, someone so kind, generous and pure—it had opened my eyes to something more. What I'd had with Stella had never been the deep, soul-catching connection I was looking for. But something told me I might have finally found what I'd been seeking in Sophie. She'd auctioned off her virtue to save her sister's life. Who does that? She's special and amazing in so many ways. And now I'm eager to get home to her.

I wonder, despite the strange master/slave start to our relationship if we have any shot at something real.

When my plane finally touches down at the hanger, I strap my leather duffle bag to my bike and take off like a bullet. The only thing on my mind is clearing my thoughts of my disastrous weekend and getting Sophie's warm, pliant body in my hands.

As my bike roars down the Pacific Coast Highway, the desire to see Sophie and to be near her rages through me. I could never have imagined that spending two nights alone after spending so many with her snuggled warmly beside me would have affected me so profoundly. But I know that it has. My brothers would say I'm going soft, and they'd be right, but I don't care.

Tearing through the mudroom, I check the kitchen and den in search of her. Finding the downstairs empty of everyone except the household staff, I take the stairs two at a time and haul ass to my bedroom, deciding it's the best possible place I could find her anyway.

Empty.

Same with the master bath. She's not here.

I call Kylie who confirms she's not working today.

What the fuck?

I try Marta next. No answer. *Has everyone just dropped off the face of the planet today?*

Unable to temper the anxiety coursing through my veins, I change into a pair of trunks and decide to swim laps and burn off this excess energy while I wait for her to get home.

I run into Beth on my way to the pool who confirms no one's seen Sophie.

Seventy-two laps later my body's tired, but my mind races on. I climb from the pool, leaving a soaking wet trail and collapse onto a lounge chair to wait. She has to come home sometime, right? Unless she already found out and she… No. She'd give me a chance to explain at least. I have to believe that.

When I open my eyes sometime later, Sophie's standing over me, her long hair falling like a wave onto my chest.

"Colton? Wake up. You're going to burn out here."

I blink several times, the harsh afternoon sunlight causing spots to dance in my eyes.

Sophie

Colton stares up at me, blinking to clear his vision. His shorts are wet and his skin is developing a golden hue. I hadn't expected him home in the middle of the day, figuring once he flew in from New York, he'd head to the office. But instead, he'd come straight home. It causes something to pinch in my chest. I want to leap into his arms, but he's still staring up at me and his mouth is tugged down into a frown.

He looks like he's been through hell and back. "What's wrong?" I ask.

He sits up and scrubs a hand across his face. "Where were you?"

"I went shopping with Marta." I point to the shopping bags I set down beside the glass patio doors.

He rises and knots the towel around his waist before stomping away.

"Colton?" I follow him. "What's wrong? Was

your trip okay?" Considering he's told me absolutely nothing, the question feels fake. I hate it.

"It was fine."

His back is to me and I place a hand against his shoulder, gently kneading the tense muscle. "Are you mad I wasn't here?"

"I like coming home to you." He shrugs.

I walk around him, so I can face him eye to eye. "You missed me."

"No. The house was too quiet. Empty."

"The housekeepers are here. You missed me."

"Can we not discuss this?" His voice is firm, but his gaze is imploring and soft. The combination causes me to melt just a little.

I suppress a smile. Knowing he missed me just as much as I missed him makes me feel giddy. "I'm home now." I link my fingers with his and his mouth relaxes into one of the smiles I'm coming to love seeing on him. "So what do you want to do now that you're back?"

His hands curl around my waist and he tugs me close. "Come swim with me."

My answering smile lights up my entire face.

He's so light and carefree — I decide I like him skipping work on a Monday. "Pool party it is. I just need to change into my bikini."

His mouth tugs up in a wicked grin. "No bikini necessary. There's no one around." He glances toward the towering green shrubs that create a virtual wall around his estate, caging it in privacy. But he's forgetting the household staff is here and the floor-to-ceiling windows mean they have a direct line of sight to the pool.

I open my mouth to protest when Colton's hands skate up the sides of my thighs, lifting my sundress to expose my black g-string panties and matching pushup bra.

He tosses the dress to a nearby chair. "Oops."

When he tugs me close, naked sun-warmed skin caresses mine and my eyes slide closed.

Feeling bold, I reach back and unclasp my bra, letting it drop away just as I feel Colton's fingers twist into the sides of my panties. He rubs his thumbs over my hip bones and slides his hands lower, pushing my panties down my legs and sending them drifting to my feet.

Being nude in the bright daylight should make me feel self-conscious, but the dark, hungry way

Colton is watching me makes me feel beautiful and special. His hands skate up my sides, sending little chill bumps over my skin despite the heat outside.

"Let's get you wet," he whispers.

Taking my hand, Colton leads me to the shallow end of the infinity pool and we wade in together, hand in hand. The water's so warm and perfect, there's no adjustment necessary as it envelopes my ankles, calves and then thighs. Though my bikini doesn't cover much, swimming naked is a completely different experience. The water licks at my skin and the resulting feeling is freeing and serene. Once we're submerged up to Colton's chest and my shoulders, he cages me in against the side of the pool and leans in to kiss me. I love kissing him. His mouth is hot and eager.

His mouth moves urgently against mine like he's chasing after something that he's desperate to reclaim something between us. I push up on my toes and wrap my arms around his neck, running my fingers through his hair.

I'm coming to realize I'm more than just a casual fuck to Colton. And I like that he's taken his time, gotten to know me, earned my trust before things progressed to a point of no return, despite the wait being maddening. Somewhere along the way, I've become addicted to the warmth he instills deep inside me, and I want more.

As hard as it is, I break our kiss, resting my forehead against his. "You haven't fucked me. Are you sleeping with someone else?" My voice is a weak whisper. But I have to know before I give myself to him. I've fallen for him completely and the knowledge that this isn't exclusive would kill me.

His determined gaze meets mine. "No. There's been no one else." He kisses my lips chastely. "I haven't fucked anyone in two years."

I let out an audible gasp. *Two years? Why?* "Vow of celibacy?" I joke.

"Something like that." His expression is somber and his jaw clenches, like he wants to say more, but doesn't.

"We could fix that..." The words linger in the humid air between us and our eyes remained locked together.

I scissor my legs around his waist and his hands move down to my ass, holding me as though I'm weightless in the water. I can feel his erection through his swim shorts and I grind against him, producing a grunt of satisfaction that murmurs deep in his throat.

He presses his hips forward, rocking slightly, the pressure against my clit maddening. In just a few short weeks, I've become addicted to his touch.

"Is that what you want, sweetness? My cock buried inside your hot little cunt?"

The friction is incredible and my eyes slip closed. "Y-yes," I admit.

Colton's fingers find my bare center and he lightly strokes me, one finger sliding against my silken heat, teasing, testing, as he moves. He circles my clit without putting direct contact there. I whimper in frustration and Colton nips at my lower lip, drawing it into his mouth and sucking.

"I want to taste you. I want to fuck you with my mouth and my fingers first. I want to make sure you're ready to handle me." He presses his cock into my center and buries his face in my neck. I love that I can feel how badly he wants me.

The need to be closer is an all-consuming desire and I wind my legs tighter around his waist as if to draw him nearer. Just the thought of how easily he'll glide into me in the warm water has me wet and ready.

With my arms planted on his shoulders, I rock against him, loving the feel of his rigid cock brushing my center and the tiny grunts he releases as he kisses my lips.

I uncross my legs from around his waist, my bare feet coming to a rest on the pool floor and I begin unlacing the string holding his swim trunks closed. Colton watches my hands work beneath the water. His tanned torso glistening with water is too inviting. I want to lick each droplet from his abs, but my goal at the moment is to have his beautiful cock in my hands.

My heart pounds unevenly as I realize this is finally it. He's not stopping me.

Realizing something other than me has captured his attention, I follow his gaze to the glass door leading into the house. Beth is standing in the open doorway looking at us.

Geez, awkward much?

"Mr. Drake…" she starts.

"Some privacy, please?" he growls shooting her an icy glare.

"But sir…"

"Get out!" he barks, but Beth doesn't retreat.

What the hell is going on?

"Mr. Drake, your wife is here," she says.

Spots dance in my vision and I sway, unsteady on my feet. A woman steps out behind Beth—tall, and regal with locks of red hair cascading down onto her shoulders and the iciest glare pointed directly at me.

Colton

I lock eyes with Stella and my erection instantly fades. She steps out onto the patio surrounding the pool and comes to an abrupt halt, realizing I'm not alone. She looks older, harsher in the broad daylight, little lines crinkle around her eyes and her mouth puckers in a frown. It was always something she was good at—frowning at me.

Her gaze collides with Sophie and I have the sudden urge to shield Sophie's body from Stella's cruel perusal—like her gaze alone will damage my sweet, pure Sophie. I glance to Sophie, who's naked, pale and trembling.

"Well, now I see what's been keeping you so busy," Stella says, her voice devoid of any emotion.

Sophie steps back away from me, the loss of her touch unwelcome and unwanted. "C-Colton?" Her shaky voice is a weak whisper.

I don't respond. I can't. All I can do it stare into the sweetest pair of blue eyes I've ever seen and pray to God she'll let me explain.

"Yes, he's married, sweetheart, so I suggest you get your naked behind out of my pool before I call the police," Stella says, placing one manicured hand against her hip.

A single tear rolls down Sophie's cheek as she moves further away from me and climbs from the pool, nude and shaking like a leaf.

My newly mended heart shatters into a million tiny pieces as everything I thought I'd gained in the last several weeks is lost again.

"Soph…" I hoist myself up over the edge of the pool and reach for her, but she jogs for the glass doors, bypassing the towels in her hurry to get away from Stella.

Fuck.

The ache in my chest intensifies. Stella's voice cuts through the dark thoughts swirling in my head.

I can't lose Sophie. There's more happening be-tween us than what either of us ever expected.

I've fallen in love with her.

Just as the thought rushes through me, I know I may have lost her already.

Filthy Beautiful Love

Available Now!

Filthy Beautiful Love

When Colton Drake paid one million dollars for Sophie Evan's virginity, the last thing he expected was to fall for her—hard—and then to watch her walk away. But when Sophie discovers that Colton has been lying to her, it is going to take more than money to get her back.

Colton won't be deterred. Sophie is his—she just doesn't know it yet. Can he seal the deal and rock her world so thoroughly she'll never want to leave again, or is it too late…

Get the emotionally charged and provocative conclusion, Filthy Beautiful Love now!

Get Two Free books

Sign up for my newsletter and I'll automatically send you two free books.

www.kendallryanbooks.com/newsletter

Follow Kendall

Website

www.kendallryanbooks.com

Facebook

www.facebook.com/kendallryanbooks

Twitter

www.twitter.com/kendallryan1

Instagram

www.instagram.com/kendallryan1

Newsletter

www.kendallryanbooks.com/newsletter

About the Author

A *New York Times*, *Wall Street Journal*, and *USA TODAY* bestselling author of more than two dozen titles, Kendall Ryan has sold over two million books, and her books have been translated into several languages in countries around the world. Her books have also appeared on the *New York Times* and *USA TODAY* bestseller list more than three dozen times. Kendall has been featured in publications such as *USA TODAY*, *Newsweek*, and *In Touch Magazine*. She lives in Texas with her husband and two sons.

To be notified of new releases or sales, join Kendall's private Mailing List.

www.kendallryanbooks.com/newsletter

Get even more of the inside scoop when you join Kendall's private Facebook group, Kendall's Kinky Cuties:

www.facebook.com/groups/kendallskinkycuties

Other Books by Kendall Ryan

Penthouse Prince
The Boyfriend Effect
My Brother's Roommate
The Stud Next Door
The Rebel
The Rival
The Rookie
The Rebound
Hot Blooded

For a complete list of Kendall's books, visit:

www.kendallryanbooks.com/all-books/

CPSIA information can be obtained
at www.ICGtesting.com
Printed in the USA
LVHW082319260622
722164LV00029B/744